My Sweet Cinderella

The Tantalising Tales Collection

Lorelei Johnson

A Cinderella Retelling

Copyright © 2020 Lorelei Johnson

All rights reserved.

The characters and events portrayed in this book are fictitious. Any similarity to real persons, living or dead, is coincidental and not intended by the author.

No part of this book may be reproduced, or stored in a retrieval system, or transmitted in any form or by any means, electronic, mechanical, photocopying, recording, or otherwise, without express written permission of the publisher.

Cover design by: Lorelei Johnson

ISBN-13: 9798542334387

PROLOGUE

The sounds of the scrubbing brush echoed through the entry hall, grating on Lucinda's nerves almost as much as the girl doing the scrubbing did. She had always been a loathsome little creature, pathetic and desperate for affection. She looked too much like her mother, the woman Lucinda's husband had never been able to forget, the woman who had always been first in his heart, followed closely by his only daughter. Lucinda had been forced to settle for third.

Third.

When she was young and naïve, she'd been determined to win him over, to claim her rightful place as first in his affections, but it soon became clear she'd set herself an impossible task. Each day her resentment grew until she couldn't stand it anymore.

When her husband came down with a sudden and mysterious illness, she thought she would finally get everything she deserved.

But he left it all to Cinderella.

That loathsome little creature was going to take everything from her, everything that Lucinda rightfully deserved. It was enough to turn her knuckles white with fury, enough to banish the thought of ever offering a semblance of affection to the child.

But she was not a child anymore.

As she stared down at the girl, it occurred to her that she had grown into quite the beauty; she had dainty features, golden hair, and though her hands were rough from years of labour, her porcelain skin refused to give up its noble status. She had curves in the right places, a cinched waist, and full lips. Cleaned up a little, she would make a beautiful lady, a beautiful princess. Her own daughters could not compare, they had unfortunately taken too much after their father.

Lucinda gripped the invitations in her hand, crumpling the expensive paper. There was no way she could allow Cinderella to go to the royal ball. She'd known the moment the invitations had arrived that she would need to find a way to keep that wretched girl away. She needed the prince to marry one of her own daughters. No one would dare look down on her if she lived in the palace, mother to the queen-to-be.

She needed to be rid of Cinderella, not just for the ball but for good. However she achieved this, she needed to avoid drawing attention. How to get rid of someone without arousing suspicion? A thought dawned on her, stretching her lips into a wicked smile.

Oh yes, she had just the thing to remove that thorn embedded in her side. She hurried to her room and scrawled a letter, before handing it to the footman and shooing him out the door. It needed to be delivered without a moment's delay. With any luck, her problem would be solved before the week was out.

The best part was, she wouldn't even need an excuse for Cinderella's sudden disappearance. Since her husband's death, few people ever visited, and none of them ever called upon Cinderella. The only thing she couldn't figure out was why she hadn't thought of it sooner.

CHAPTER 1

Cinderella

The house had been buzzing with excitement for a few days, ever since the messenger arrived and placed four envelopes into Cinderella's hands. Her stepmother had snatched them away, clearly expecting their arrival, and ignored Cinderella's questions.

It was clear by her stepmother's secretive behaviour and the way she and her stepsisters, Prudence and Gertrude, stopped twittering as soon as she entered the room that her stepmother didn't want her to know what was in those letters.

Though her stepmother was cunning and tight lipped when she wanted to be, her daughters hadn't yet mastered that craft. Neither of them were particularly subtle creatures. Besides that, the paper had been of the finest quality and messenger himself was pristine and wearing the royal crest quite clearly on his coat. And she also knew the prince's birthday was coming up, she had heard the tittle tattle of other servants at the market, so she knew perfectly well what it was her stepmother was trying to hide.

A royal ball was being held in a little over a month.

It was officially to celebrate Prince Henri's twenty-fifth birthday, however, unofficially there were whispers of matchmaking. It was no secret that the king wanted his son to marry, and every eligible lady in the kingdom had been invited, some had even been invited from other kingdoms, or so the gossip said. The king was clearly getting desperate.

Cinderella wondered what it would be like to attend. She knew her stepmother's eye was on Prince Henri, but she didn't care about that. She longed to attend her first ball, to dance in a room full of ball gowns that sparkled like jewels, to feel, just for one night, like the lady her mother had always wanted her to be. Maybe she'd meet someone, fall in love, maybe this would be her chance to have the family she'd longed for since the death of her parents.

She could confront her stepmother in hopes that she would give in when it became clear Cinderella knew her game. Surely it wouldn't be so bad to let her go to a ball, she'd never asked her stepmother for anything. It wasn't as if she was likely to catch the eye of the prince, so it shouldn't matter.

Cinderella sighed. Her stepmother would never allow it. It delighted Lucinda too much to say no to Cinderella. Anything she asked of her would be denied, it was why she never asked for anything. Her stepmother made no secret of the fact that she detested Cinderella, although Cinderella wasn't sure what she had done to earn her disdain.

Could she steal her invitation and sneak into the ball?

No, that wouldn't work either. She had nothing to wear. If she took one of her stepsisters' dresses there would be hell to pay. Besides, none of them would fit her. It was hopeless.

'Cinderella!' Prudence screeched from the room atop the stairs.

'Cinderella!' Gertrude screeched even louder, if that were at all possible.

The neighbourhood dogs began to bark and howl at the noise they were making. Another sigh passed Cinderella's lips as she put down the broom and wiped her hands on her apron. She headed up to the room to find her stepsisters seated, waiting for her to begin their beauty treatments.

Cinderella didn't know why they insisted on these bizarre treatments. The ointments often smelled like feet and they took an awful amount of time to take effect, although Cinderella was yet to see any improvement to their complexions and suspected that the treatments were never going to work.

'Make sure you do it properly, Cinderella,' Prudence said. 'You have obviously been doing it wrong, my complexion hasn't improved nearly as much as it should have.'

'Honestly, how do you expect us to get the prince's attention if we look as plain as you?' Gertrude sniped.

No amount of ointment would fix their bone structure or their personalities. Cinderella kept that thought to herself as she smeared the ointment on Gertrude's face. She took some satisfaction in the fact that it probably contained someone's foot shavings and beetle guts. Perhaps if her stepsisters worked on their inner beauty, it would reflect outwardly.

'What are you smiling about?' Prudence snapped.

'Nothing,' Cinderella said innocently and smeared the ointment on her sister's skin.

She doubted either of them would get the outcome they were hoping for. There were many beautiful women in the kingdom, much more beautiful than any in their house. And it wasn't as if her stepsisters could charm him with their wit.

She couldn't understand why they would want to marry the prince anyway. He was handsome, sure, she'd seen him at some public event or other. He'd been handsome when they'd met some fifteen years ago, but in a boyish way. Now he had the rugged charm of a man, and there were not many women in the kingdom who could refuse that charm. There were plenty of scandals surrounding him, once upon a time, though the rumours seemed to have died down. The playboy prince seemed to have settled, but had he really? Perhaps he had simply become more skilled at covering his tracks.

But handsomeness aside, being a princess, always in the spotlight, didn't appeal to Cinderella. She'd much prefer a quite country life, with a good man who loved her as her father had loved her mother. She didn't mind if they were rich or poor, though she hoped she could live up to her mother's wishes and lead a life she would have been proud of.

'What are you daydreaming about? Stupid girl. Wash it off,' Prudence's voice dragged her out of her thoughts like nails on a chalkboard.

It would be nice to have a family that actually thought of her as family, instead of an indentured servant. She set about washing the foul-smelling gunk from her sisters' faces when the doorbell rang.

'Don't you dare,' Prudence said.

'Lucinda would have our heads if I don't,' Cinderella pointed out.

Prudence gave an unladylike snort as she conceded and Cinderella raced to the door, glad for the moment's reprieve from her stepsisters. She opened it to reveal a stern looking woman. Her hair was dark and pulled back tightly beneath her hat, her plump body was dressed finely but it was clearly the clothes of a servant. Cinderella couldn't see a crest anywhere, but she clearly worked for a very wealthy family.

'Can I help you?' Cinderella asked politely, plastering a warm smile onto her face.

The woman looked down her pointed nose at Cinderella, her hawk-like eyes scrutinising every detail before she finally sniffed. 'I'm here to see Lady Tremaine. She is expecting me.'

'Of course,' Cinderella said, as if she knew exactly what the woman was talking about, even though she had no idea. The woman terrified her, so she decided not to ask any questions. Lucinda would likely punish her later but better the devil you know.

Cinderella showed the woman into the parlour and before she could offer tea, Lucinda entered the room gracefully. Lucinda always waited for Cinderella to fetch her when she had guests, she said it was important for appearances, so it was strange that she had come almost instantly to see this servant. No matter what house they came from, Lucinda would always see herself as better than a servant. Her stepmother was up to something and a bad feeling began to settle in Cinderella's stomach.

Lucinda closed the door behind her, a clear indication that Cinderella was to stay in the room. Another peculiarity.

'Madam Dubois, so good of you to come on such short notice,' Lucinda said courteously. She took a seat opposite the woman and Cinderella was left to stand awkwardly off to the side.

'Is this the girl?' Madam Dubois asked.

'Yes. I was so relieved to hear you had an...opening.' Lucinda was trying to hide her smile, but she looked like a cat cornering a canary.

'Hmm...' Madam Dubois said, standing from her chair and circling Cinderella like a vulture.

What was Lucinda up to? Was she going to send her to work somewhere else? Send her away from her family home to live god knows where? She would expect money to be sent back, no doubt. Although even if money was tight, it would have made more sense for Cinderella to stay and work, as she had been expected to since her father died, for free.

If not that, then what?

'Strip,' Madam Dubois ordered.

'I beg your pardon?' Cinderella asked, certain she must have misheard the woman.

Fury flashed in Lucinda's eyes. 'You heard her, stupid girl. Strip.'

Cinderella looked from Lucinda to Madam Dubois, both women simply stared impatiently back at her. 'But...why?'

Lucinda's scowl deepened and Cinderella felt like a deer caught in a hunter's sights. With shaking hands she began unfastening her dress. She pushed it slowly off her shoulders, down her arms, hoping that at any point one of them would tell her to stop.

They didn't.

The dress pooled around her feet and she stood before them in nothing but her slip. Her arms wrapped around her chest in a vain attempt to hide her exposed body.

'All of it,' Madam Dubois ordered.

Cinderella's mouth dropped open. She looked again at her stepmother. She didn't know why she'd looked at Lucinda, it wasn't like she had ever come to her rescue in the past. Lucinda stared coldly at her and Cinderella swallowed hard, trying to keep back the tears that were pricking at her eyes as she slid off the last bit of fabric covering her body. She shivered as the cool air touched her skin and folded her arms over her chest once more.

Madam Dubois clicked her tongue loudly in frustration and pulled her arms down to her sides. Tears welled in Cinderella's eyes as Madama Dubois began her vulture circling again. Her fingers poked and prodded parts of her body as she hummed in consideration. A tear dripped onto Cinderella's cheek and she hastily wiped it away.

'She's a little thin,' Madam Dubois said.

'Easily rectified, I'm sure,' Lucinda said with a smile.

The way they spoke about her was like they were talking about purchasing a goat, Cinderella would have been appalled except that she saw Madam Dubois nod at her to get dressed and she was too preoccupied with covering herself to think about anything else.

'I'll give you twenty for her,' Madam Dubois said.

Twenty? Her stepmother was really selling her off?

Lucinda's smile turned triumphant and she shook the woman's hand.

'You do understand that if she is…let go, you are expected to take her back into your employ,' Madam Dubois said.

Employ? As if Lucinda had actually employed her, she hadn't paid her a cent. This was her home, this was where she grew up, this was where her parents raised her to be a lady. How ashamed they would be to see her now.

Lucinda didn't seem at all pleased to hear this but she nodded tightly. 'Of course.'

Madam Dubois handed over a handful of gold coins and the transaction was complete. 'I will give you five minutes to collect your things, girl. Do not keep me waiting.' With that, the woman headed out of the room.

'Stepmother, you can't do this!' Cinderella protested.

A sharp slap echoed through the room, leaving a throbbing sting in its wake. Cinderella pressed her hand to her cheek, tears spilling from her eyes. 'I think you'll find I just did. Now go outside and tell Madam Dubois that you have nothing to pack. If you never set foot in this house again, it will be too soon.'

'What did I ever do to make you hate me so much?' Cinderella asked, the question she'd long asked herself tumbling out of her mouth.

'You were born.'

CHAPTER 2

Henri

Henri pulled his wrist back as he aimed, then let the dart fly. He smiled triumphantly as it hit the bullseye, expecting the click of his friend's tongue as he furthered his lead. It was all good-natured fun, though Henri couldn't help feeling that the only reason his friend, William Dansbury, insisted on playing anymore was because the more he lost, the more he wanted to win. He imagined if that win ever happened, it would be the most unsportsmanlike victory the kingdom had ever known.

'I heard another one of your sex slaves has been let go,' William said as he lined up his next shot.

'Don't call them that. You make me sound like a rapist,' Henri said.

Henri honestly wasn't sure how long it had been

going on now. It had all started as some fooling around with a few noble ladies, a few minor scandals, and his father had gone to Madam Dubois with his tomato-red face after Henri had refused to repent and demanded that she fix it.

Henri wasn't sure how she was going to do that but she came up with a plan that intrigued him. He was barely twenty at the time, and when she had said she would bring women for his amusement, it sounded just fine to him.

But nearly five years later, it was losing its lustre, and yet Madam Dubois kept bringing these girls to him. It had been fun in the beginning, but it was all becoming unfulfilling now. At first, he hadn't known the details, but he'd picked them up over the years, bits and pieces from various girls. They were, in fact, purchased for his amusement, so William's assessment of them was more accurate that he would like.

'They are women procured for your particular…amusement. They are not paid a wage, and you fuck them. What else should I call them?'

Even as William's bluntness sometimes irked him, it was also the reason they were such good friends. He was quite possibly the only person in the kingdom who treated him just like anyone else. Except when Henri pulled rank, which wasn't very often.

'I don't do anything they don't want.'

'Just because they like it doesn't mean they aren't sex slaves,' William teased. 'Why don't you just marry already?'

'Why buy the cow when the milk is free?' Henri asked, flashing a devilish smile. But the words themselves were empty bravado. The real reason he hadn't married was simply because he'd never met a woman he wanted to marry. They were all the same, simpering ladies who cared only for money and status. Some of them were boring, only there because their parents insisted, they knew nothing of the world and didn't care to. Others were cunning, or tried to be, they were there for the power, they were the ones looking twenty years ahead, their eyes firmly on the throne. And, of course, anyone of lower birth was not an option.

'You could have any number of beautiful women with a single question,' William continued, a hint of envy in his tone.

'Beauty isn't everything,' Henri said.

'You want to know what I think?'

'No.'

'I think the only reason you haven't chosen a wife is to piss off your father,' William said.

'That's an added perk,' Henri admitted. His father was pushing so hard for him to marry, using every trick he could find. He would have forced a betrothal by now if he thought it would stick, but the prince backing out of an engagement was not good politics. 'Why are you pushing this? It's not as if you have a wife.'

'Two reasons. One,' William said, raising a single finger for emphasis, 'I'm not a prince. Two,' he continued, raising a second finger, 'all the eligible women in this kingdom are waiting for you. So do the men of this country a favour and pick one already.'

The two of them laughed at the joke, though both of them knew it was true.

William had been Henri's friend for as long as he could remember. He was the only one who treated him like everyone else, but there had been another once before. When his mother passed almost fifteen years ago. He'd met a girl in the cemetery and she had spoken to him as if he were anyone else. At first he thought she didn't know who he was but she knew, it just hadn't seemed to matter to her.

Why was he remembering her now?

William took his final shot, missing the bullseye completely and ending the game with another victory to Henri. 'Enough darts, I can't take the crushing defeat anymore,' William said. 'So, do I get the sordid details of the most recent woman?'

Henri rolled his eyes. 'What sordid details? She fell in love with me, so she said. I honestly doubt these girls know what love is.'

'Correction, you don't know what love is and you're projecting that cynicism onto them,' William said.

A carriage rattled up the drive, both men looked out the window as it approached. Henri knew instantly what it was and supressed the sigh that came to his lips. William, on the other hand, looked like a child in a toy store.

'Oh, the new one has arrived,' he said excitedly and moved to get a closer look. Henri grudgingly did the same.

Madam Dubois exited the carriage first, the usual stern look on her face. He hoped that by now she was also tiring of the process. She tapped her foot impatiently on the cobblestones as she waited for the unlucky girl to exit.

The woman who followed was not at all what Henri had been expecting. She certainly looked like a maid, the kind who was used to hard work, with her plain dress, scuffed shoes, and the soot dusting her skin. But her shoulders were squared, her head held high, as if she were born a noble lady, not a gutter snipe. Her eyes were red, like she'd been holding back tears and he wondered how it was she had come to be there. It was the first time he'd ever asked that question of any of the women Madam Dubois had brought him over the years.

'I bet she's a real beauty once she's cleaned up a little,' William said, seemingly in awe of the new arrival and something unpleasant stirred in Henri's chest, something almost possessive.

What was that?

'I suppose,' he said instead, not wanting to give anything away. He was probably just in a strange mood after hearing about the upcoming ball. His father's latest matchmaking scheme.

'You have no appreciation for anything. I blame that golden spoon in your mouth,' William said, rolling his eyes. 'Shame she's not nobility.'

'You want her?' Henri asked, raising his eyebrows.

'Are you offering?'

'No.' He hadn't meant to say the word out loud. It had rolled off his tongue almost before it entered his mind. There was something familiar about her but he couldn't quite put his finger on it. He was certain they had never met before. Perhaps she reminded him of someone?

'I always knew you were the kid that didn't share your toys,' William said.

Madam Dubois led the woman inside and Henri was surprised to find that he was actually eager to meet this one. But he couldn't let anyone know that. He would wait, he would summon her in the evening and find out if there was anything behind this feeling or if it was all his imagination.

For the first time in a long time, Henri was actually looking forward to something.

CHAPTER 3

Cinderella

Cinderella left the house, as she had been told, without a single possession. No mementos of her mother or father, nothing from her childhood. It was clear that her Stepmother thought everything in that house belonged to her and Cinderella was entitled to none of it. How could her father have loved someone so cruel?

She bit the inside of her cheek to keep from crying as she exited the house, and Madam Dubois looked her over with an arched eyebrow, but she remained silent, for which Cinderella was grateful.

The woman ushered her into the carriage and slammed the door shut behind them. The coachman began the journey to whatever big house had just bought her. She still had no idea what was going on.

'Pay attention, girl. I don't like repeating myself,' Madam Dubois said. Cinderella sat up and did her best to look at the woman. If this was her new situation, there was no sense in making enemies. At least until she could find a way out of this.

'First and foremost, what happens at the palace stays at the palace, do you understand? If any rumours begin to circulate, it's straight to the dungeons.'

Cinderella blinked in surprise. 'I'm sorry, did you say palace?'

Had she been sold to the royal family? She would have thought that of all the places in the kingdom, the palace would not be keeping slaves. And yet, here she was, in a royal carriage after being bought for a mere twenty gold coins. Who would have thought a person's life could be valued by a handful of coins?

If they found out she was nobility, what would they do to her? Would they silence her in some awful way? Send her some place no one would ever find her? Her options were looking bleaker by the second.

'I told you to pay attention,' Madam Dubois said stiffly. 'Do you understand what I just said?'

'Yes, Madam,' Cinderella said meekly.

'Good. You will be provided with good lodgings, new clothes, and your duties will be fairly straight forward. I don't know why you look so miserable. You're about to enter into a very good life for someone of your ilk,' Madam Dubois continued. 'And it won't be forever. Trust me on that, you will be sent back soon enough, or you will be elevated within the palace, given a good wage.'

Cinderella's brow furrowed with questions but she wasn't sure she should ask them. Why would they look after a slave so well? What was it they expected of her exactly?

The palace loomed over them as the carriage approached. Cinderella could hardly keep her mouth closed. She'd seen the palace from a distance before but never up close. It was enormous. It must take a hundred people to run it. It seemed a ridiculous thing for a family of two.

The carriage stopped and Madam Dubois stepped out. Cinderella's stomach fluttered like there were tiny birds in there. The longer she waited, the sterner Madam Dubois' face grew. She swallowed hard and followed her new mistress onto the palace grounds.

In the kitchens, servants were busily working away but they all stopped to look at her as she entered. The knowing looks on their faces told her they knew something she did not and she began to feel shy under their gaze.

'What is your name?' Madam Dubois hissed under her breath.

'Cinderella.'

'This is Cinderella. Where is Esther?' Madam Dubois began. Someone pointed a general direction, which seemed to tell Madam Dubois everything she needed to know. 'Wait here,' she said before stalking in the direction that Esther presumably was.

Cinderella shuffled on her feet as she looked around. It was impossible to ignore their stares, the whispering. Colour began to rise in her cheeks when a woman approached her with an expression like she'd swallowed something bitter. She stood in front of Cinderella, arms folded across her chest as she looked down her nose.

It seemed that everywhere she went people hated her. Was there something wrong with her? Maybe she subconsciously had a horrible look on her face? How would she know that?

'So, you're the new one,' the woman sneered.

'I suppose so,' Cinderella said uncertainly. She still wasn't sure what her role here was exactly.

'They'll let anyone in these days,' she said with a roll of her eyes.

'It isn't like I chose to be here,' Cinderella said before she could stop herself.

The woman raised an eyebrow at her as if she couldn't believe Cinderella had dared to speak to her. 'Well, you don't look like much,' she said, flicking her eyes over Cinderella. 'He'll tire of you quickly.'

He?

Madam Dubois suddenly appeared behind the awful woman, a stern frown on her brow. 'Not as quickly as he tired of you, Bethany. Now get out of my sight before I send you packing,' she snapped.

Cinderella blinked in surprise. Had Madam Dubois

just defended her? Perhaps she had misjudged the woman. Or perhaps she just disliked Bethany. That seemed the more plausible scenario.

Another woman appeared behind Madam Dubois. She had a kind face and a warm smile, the first bit of kindness Cinderella had seen in a long time. 'Esther will get you cleaned up and properly attired. Then we can begin,' Madam Dubois said.

Esther took Cinderella's hand. 'Come on, you'll feel like nobility when I'm done with you,' she said.

If only she knew that Cinderella already was nobility. But she said nothing and let Esther led her to a bathroom. It was nicer than the bathroom at home, and yet meant for servants. Her stepmother would have a fit if she saw it.

'Alright, in you get,' Esther said.

Cinderella looked at the tub full of warm water that gently wafted steam through the cool air. She did want to get in but she had already been naked in front of enough people for one day. She waited for Esther to leave but the woman made no move to go.

'You are an innocent little thing, aren't you?' Esther said gently. 'You will have to get used to people seeing you naked. I have to help you clean.'

'I can do it myself,' Cinderella said.

Esther shook her head with a sad smile and Cinderella sighed. There was no other option, then. She stripped for the second time that day in front of a total stranger and stepped into the tub.

Esther lathered her hair in lavender shampoo but remained silent. Cinderella wasn't sure if she preferred her to be silent or to speak, it felt awkward. 'What am I here for?' Cinderella finally asked.

'Madam Dubois will tell you soon,' Esther said.

'Is it something dreadful? I can't see how it can be good if no one will talk about it.'

'It's not all bad, I promise. You will be treated better than any other member of staff while you are in this…role.'

Cinderella didn't find that particularly comforting. With a final rinse, she was finally clean enough to satisfy Esther, and she smelled like she'd just rolled around in a lavender bush, which seemed a bit extreme.

Ester helped her into new undergarments that were made of the softest fabric she'd ever touched, and into a corset, which she instantly hated, though Esther mused that she didn't have to pull it too tight as she was already so thin. Cinderella supposed most women would be happy with that assessment, but then, most women weren't thin because they'd had their meals rationed for years to the point that they never truly felt full.

The dress that Esther put her in was a beautiful gown. Though it was still a simple design befitting someone of lower rank, the blue was brilliant and deep, an obviously expensive shade, and the cut was perfect, accentuating her figure.

The further into this process she got, the more suspicious she became. What on Earth was going on?

Once she was deemed appropriately presentable, Esther took her back to Madam Dubois. The woman looked her over, circling like a vulture once more before finally giving a tight nod of approval. 'Yes, he will like you.'

'Who will?'

Madam Dubois clicked her tongue in irritation. 'You will be serving the prince for the foreseeable future. Everything he asks, you will do, understood?'

'Yes, Madam,' Cinderella said obediently. She felt the tension in her heart lift a little. Serving the prince? Would he remember her? No, that didn't' seem likely. She had changed and he met so many people every day.

Either way, he would surely treat her better than her stepmother ever did. She wasn't sure why serving him meant she needed such a nice dress, but she was happy to wear it. She felt more like the lady she was supposed to be than she had since her father died.

Still, she couldn't help quietly fuming at the injustice of it, at her stepmother's selfishness. She was a Lady, forced to act like a servant and now she had been sold as a slave. Why did her stepmother hate her so much? How was she allowed to get away with such cruelty?

'Quickly, now. I'll show you only once. Mistakes are not tolerated here,' Madam Dubois said as she walked briskly down the hallway.

Cinderella squared her shoulders with determination. She would do her best until she figured out how to get out of there. Things looked bleak now but her father always told her that things had a way of working out if you only put in the effort.

She held onto those words tightly as tears pricked at her eyes.

It would work out if she only put in the effort.

CHAPTER 4

Cinderella

The day had passed so quickly, and yet it felt like a week. There was so much to take in, so much to learn. Madam Dubois had given her a tour of the palace, as if she should remember the layout instantly, but Cinderella knew that she was going to get lost, probably for three months at least. She wondered how anyone could remember the layout of such an enormous building. She was sure that if her house was that big, she would have to carry around a blueprint.

Maybe she could get a blueprint? Doubtful. Other than it being a security risk, she was sure that no one would go out of their way to give her one. She doubted anyone would go out of their way to do anything for her in this place.

She had only one job, it seemed, which was serve

the prince, though it seemed like there was something about it no one was willing to tell her. But there was something else she would have to do during her time at the palace, and that was avoid Bethany. The woman had done nothing but glare at her all day, unable to do anything else with Madam Dubois so close. She dreaded to think what might happen if Bethany caught her alone.

The room she'd been given was simple but better than the attic her stepmother forced her to sleep in. She was surprised that she was given a room to herself, but Madam Dubois explained that it was because the prince could call on her day or night and she didn't want it to disturb the other staff. It made sense, though she couldn't help feeling bitter that she was the only one who would have to suffer through broken sleep.

She eyed the golden bell in the corner of the room. It glinted beautifully in the candlelight as if it were not an evil device that was going to ruin her sleep. How often would he really use it? How often would he actually call for her late at night? Obviously often enough to warrant her having her own room.

She sighed.

She still hadn't actually met the prince yet, she had no idea what to expect from him. She couldn't help wondering if that boy she met at the cemetery all those years ago was in there somewhere or if he had changed completely.

As if he knew that she was thinking about him, the golden bell finally started to ring. She watched it for a moment, her stomach flipping nervously. What would he want from her at this time of night? There was no one who she could ask for help if she needed it, everyone had already gone to bed.

It wasn't like ignoring it was going to be any better. She let out a resigned sigh and headed to the prince's room. Was it possible to sigh oneself to death? She shook her head, trying to dislodge her dreary thoughts and focus on the task at hand. She knew her way to the prince's room because it was the only place Madam Dubois had ensured she knew, she'd even tested her on it. But if she didn't pay attention to where she was going, she would definitely get lost.

She took a few deep breaths as she stood in front of the door, then swallowed hard before raising her hand to the varnished wood. Her knock was more timid than she had expected, so she tried again and waited for the muffled sound of his voice to bid her entry.

She hadn't been inside the room before, and it was the epitome of luxury, as one would expect. She didn't have time to take in her surroundings because standing in the firelight, leaning against the mantle, was the prince. He turned slowly toward her as she entered and her eyes drank him in; dancing fingers of light and shadow trailed across the muscled contours of his shirtless torso and the eyes gazing at her from behind locks of blonde hair were predatory. She'd never seen a man like this before. She pulled her eyes away but she wasn't sure where to look instead. Finally, she settled for the floor.

The prince chuckled in amusement and a blush rose to her cheeks. She couldn't bring herself to look at him, she was afraid of staring, again, but also afraid that he would laugh at her. Why wasn't he wearing a shirt? He'd surely done that on purpose.

'You called for me, my lord?' she said, still staring at the floor.

'I did,' he answered and though she waited, he offered nothing else. He walked towards her and circled her in much the same way that Madam Dubois had before purchasing her. Cinderella blushed more deeply, her face felt so hot she must actually be glowing. Would he demand that she strip, too?

Surely not.

Cinderella glanced up, unable to help herself, and her eyes met the prince's hungry gaze.

'You seem very innocent,' he said, his voice sending a shudder through her and her heart began to race.

'Were you expecting someone older or loose in morals?' Cinderella responded, the words rolling off her tongue before she could clamp her mouth shut.

The corners of his lips twisted up in amusement but he didn't offer an answer. Instead, he took a strand of her hair, running his fingers along the golden lock, his eyes never leaving hers. There was a tension in the air that crackled like electricity, prickling her skin in nervous anticipation. Her breath hitched in her throat.

She wasn't so naïve that she didn't realise what he was doing, but no man had ever flirted with her before, and this man owned her. What was she supposed to do in this situation?

'What's your name?' he asked.

'Cinderella, my lord.'

He moved behind her and she could feel the warmth of him at her back. He placed his hands on her waist and pulled her into him. 'Cinderella,' he whispered, his lips close to her ear and she shivered involuntarily. He took her ear between his teeth and a gasp escaped her lips as a warmth ignited in her core. She'd never felt anything like it, it felt blissfully wrong.

She struggled against him, trying to break free. It didn't matter how good it felt, she shouldn't be doing this. He shouldn't be doing this. But he only pulled her harder against him, as though her gasp were a sign that he had won.

Maybe he had.

Cinderella swallowed hard as his lips moved away from her ear and trailed down her neck. A tingling sensation began to build between her legs and a moan escaped her. Her cheeks flushed with embarrassment.

'Now that is a good sound,' the prince whispered, his voice low and alluring. His hand slid slowly down her body, coming closer and closer to her core.

No. She couldn't allow this to go any further.

Maybe she was just a slave now but she was a lady and he had no right to touch her as he pleased.

Coming to her senses, Cinderella struggled free and before she knew what was happening, a loud slap echoed through the air. The prince stared at her and she at him for a long moment, as if neither of them registered exactly what had happened. Her hand was still floating in the air and she quickly snatched it to her chest.

Had she just slapped the prince? Oh God, she was going to end up locked in a dungeon or flogged. Maybe he'd just send her home, that wouldn't be so bad.

The prince looked at her questioningly before bursting into laughter, his eyes shining brightly with amusement. 'So, you would strike your master?'

Cinderella had expected him to be furious, but there was no hint of anger in his voice. For some reason, that scared her more. 'I-I...' she didn't know how to explain her actions. Clearly, this is what she had been purchased for. She was no fool; she knew she had no rights here, knew that he could help himself to whatever part of her he felt entitled to. But the part of her that had once been a lady couldn't just stand there and let him take her.

Though, disturbingly, there was also a part of her that wanted to do just that.

What was wrong with her?

He grabbed her wrist and pulled her to him. His

scent enveloped her as he held her gaze with his beautiful green eyes, trapping her. She couldn't look away from him, couldn't think straight with her heart hammering in her chest.

'Let's make a bet, my sweet Cinderella,' he said, amusement dancing on his lips.

'A bet?'

'Yes. There is going to be a ball here at the palace in one month. If I can't get you to fall in love with me by then, you are free to leave.'

Free? Just like that? All she had to do was not fall in love with him. That should be easy enough, shouldn't it?

'How will you know if I've lost the bet?' she asked hesitantly. She wasn't very good at lying but she might do it if it meant gaining her freedom. After all, it wasn't like she had put herself in this situation.

He smirked. 'Your face is so open it's almost indecent. I'll know.'

She flushed, glaring down at the floor. Her stepsisters had teased her for being unable to hide her emotions, enjoying the way their small cruelties had so easily provoked expressions of hurt and despair. She could never hide an emotion like love. Not that she was worried about losing.

'If I agree to this,' she began slowly, 'I don't want to spend the next month as some sort of... concubine. Will you promise not to touch me?'

'No,' he said without hesitation, his eyes hungry

and predatory. 'But,' he said, leaning in until his face was only inches from hers, 'I promise I won't do anything you don't want me to. Which won't leave much off limits by the end of the month.'

His confidence was unnerving – she was sure he had skilfully seduced countless women before her. But those were probably the best terms she could hope for. Surely she could find a way to fend him off for a month. Maybe she could avoid him entirely for most of that time.

'And if you win?' she asked, waiting for the other shoe to drop. What would he ask of her for such a generous boon? It was probably something completely awful.

'Then you will be mine until I say otherwise.'

Cinderella's brow furrowed in confusion. Didn't he already have that? Was this some kind of sadistic game for him? He was toying with her. But what choice did she have? This was her first chance at actual freedom. If she didn't agree to it, she was his. If she did, she at least had a chance.

It seemed too good to be true, too easy, but she wasn't going to look a gift horse in the mouth. All she had to do was not fall in love with this pompous, sadistic prince. For the first time in a long time, a smile stretched her lips. 'Alright, deal. If there's nothing else, my Lord – '

'Oh, you can't leave just yet. I have a reputation to uphold,' the prince said, smiling wickedly.

'I don't understand,' Cinderella said, all confidence drained from her voice.

'You will sleep here tonight.'

'What?'

'Clothed or naked, whatever you prefer.' He flashed that wicked smile of his again and Cinderella's heart pounded loudly in her chest.

'C-clothed,' she said and wrapped her arms defensively around herself. She would have to fend him off the whole night? She needed a plan. She needed a defence.

The prince gestured to the bed and Cinderella walked slowly towards it. There had to be a way out of this. There had to be something. 'I-I could just sleep on the chair by the fire, no one would know the difference,' she said quickly.

'I would,' Henri said, his voice a low rumble accentuated by that devilish smile.

She swallowed hard and he gestured towards the bed again. How was she supposed to spend the whole night in a bed with him?

'Do I need to tie you up? That can be arranged,' he said.

'No!' she blurted out and nervously got into the bed. She laid there in the most comfortable bed she had ever felt and was stiff as a corpse. Her chest felt tight. What was she going to do?

She felt the prince get in next to her but she couldn't bring herself to look at him. He sighed.

'Could you be any more unsexy?' he asked.

Cinderella looked over at him but his eyes were closed. Unsexy? Irritation boiled in her but she bit her tongue to keep from saying anything. The sooner this prince went to sleep, the better.

The prince slid his arm around her and pulled her to him.

'Hey!' Cinderella protested, as she tried to wriggle free. Her heart hammered in her chest. What was he playing at? But the prince didn't answer, he simply tightened his grip on her.

'Stop fidgeting, woman,' he muttered.

Her body went stiff again. He was right, she needed to be still. The sooner he went to sleep, the sooner she could free herself and go to her own bed. In her ear, she could hear his deep, gentle breathing. He was asleep already? But his grip was still so tight on her. How was she supposed to escape now? One thing was for certain, she wouldn't be sleeping much that night.

CHAPTER 5

Henri

Prince Henri's eyes slowly opened as the morning light poured into the room. He couldn't remember the last time he'd slept so well, though the reason for it seemed to have disappeared at some point. Cinderella was no longer in his bed.

Curious.

She was the first to sneak away, the first to refuse him so boldly, the first woman to ever slap him. He chuckled to himself. She was certainly amusing.

She was also certainly a virgin.

Madam Dubois had brought them from time to time. She always seemed most proud of those finds, as if he would be pleased to have an innocent girl to ruin. There was a reason virgins didn't last long and it wasn't because they'd lost that title. It wasn't exactly a mantle he wanted to hang on his wall. He'd sooner go to a brothel, though his father would never allow it, which only made it all the more appealing.

No, he typically kept the virgins around long enough to keep up appearances, then sent them home with a promise not to say a word. He had a reputation to uphold, after all. As far as he knew, none of them had ever said anything. Most had been grateful, some had been disappointed, he didn't really care. He hadn't cared about much of anything for a long time now.

Cinderella was different, though. There was something about her. She looked so innocent and meek, yet there was a fire in her, a spark that could be nurtured into something more. Although, he supposed fire in a servant was not especially appealing to most masters. Still, he couldn't help wanting to bring it out to see what she was made of.

The bet had been a spur of the moment decision, he was curious to see how she'd react, what tactics she would try to employ to win. Her freedom was on the line, or so she thought. He wondered how hard she would fight for it.

Clearly one of her tactics was to stay away from him as much as possible. Smart, but he wasn't going to make it that easy for her. A knock at the door and a muffled voice made him sigh. He didn't need to make out the words to know what it was about. He was expected to have breakfast with his father, again.

He forced himself out of bed and pulled on some

clothes. His relationship with his father had been strained since his mother died. They'd been happy before that but once she was gone, his father changed. Suddenly Henri's life had become all about preparing for life as king. Lessons and etiquette and practice. Nothing was ever good enough. And when he turned twenty, the pressure was on to find him a wife, though it was clear that his father wasn't interested in letting him choose one for himself. Henri had stubbornly refused all of the women presented to him, mostly out of spite, but also because he wasn't ready to be married.

If he married a woman that he loved as much as his father loved his mother, would he turn into the same shell of a man if she died? He didn't want that life for himself.

The dining table was set as it usually was, with the king at the head of the table and Henri's setting a few seats down, as if the distance between them needed to be emphasised. He took his seat in front of the empty plate. His father had already started eating, he was the king and he waited for no one, not even his son.

How long would it take him today?

Henri put a forkful of eggs into his mouth and the king seemed to take that as his cue to begin.

'Have you gone to the tailor yet?'

'What for?'

'The ball,' the king replied, irritation clear on his face.

He was right, Henri was well aware why he was supposed to go to the tailor, he was playing dumb for no reason. Well, not no reason, he was hoping his father would drop it, or at the very least he was hoping to agitate him, which was working.

'You know this one is special,' the king said, visibly making an effort to calm his temper.

'Why is it any different from any other birthday?' Henri asked. 'You will push women at me and hope I choose to marry one of them and I will stubbornly refuse. So is it really necessary to have a new suit made?'

'It is your duty as heir to the throne,' the king said through gritted teeth.

'I'll not chain myself to some harpy for the rest of my life just because it's my duty.'

'You will do as I command,' the king snapped his face turning red.

'Are you speaking as my king or my father?'

Silence rang through the dining room and when it became clear that his father was not going to answer the question, Henri put his cutlery on the table. He stood, inclined his head half-heartedly and with his hands balled into fists at his side, he left his father to fume over his breakfast.

His father was getting more and more impatient with him, more insistent on his finding a wife. How long until he tried to force the matter, until he chose a wife for him and left Henri with no alternative?

For some reason, Cinderella's face popped into his head. She could surely cheer him up. At the very least, she should be able to take his mind off things for a while. He went back to his room and rung the bell for her.

He was dreading the upcoming ball now. He knew how his father would arrange it. Every eligible lady in the kingdom would be there and even some from other kingdoms. They'd be presented to him formally, individually, giving him time to look them over in the hopes that he would fall madly in love at first sight with one of them.

A ridiculous notion.

His father clearly forgot that Henri had met many beautiful women in his life, and he had already learnt that beauty wasn't everything. He could hardly be expected to sight a girl from across the room and decide she was the one. What fairy tales had the king been reading to form such an idea?

He looked at the door. She should be here by now, what was keeping her?

He rang the bell again, impatience fanning the flames of his temper.

He began to pace in front of the fireplace. There had to be a way out of this marriage thing. Maybe if his father just backed off, he'd actually be happy with the idea of finding someone to spend the rest of his life with. That was never going to happen.

He let out a frustrated growl. Where was that girl?

Was she ignoring him? The audacity of her, ignoring a summons from her prince. Bet or no bet, he would not have that. He would show her that disobedience would not go unpunished. He stormed out of his room, down the hall towards the servants' quarters.

If this was how she wanted to play then game on.

CHAPTER 6

Cinderella

Somehow, Prince Henri had garnered the nickname Prince Charming. Cinderella could think of a hundred names that suited him better, none of them quite so pleasant. The little boy she remembered from the cemetery fifteen years ago had grown into someone she didn't recognise. Perhaps she had too.

She sighed. Maybe it was better this way.

As she walked back to her room through the servants' quarters, all eyes were on her. Some were full of pity, some full of jealously, some full of disdain. She tried to ignore the whispers swirling around her. She tried to ignore Bethany's furious glare even as it felt like a hole was being burnt into her head.

I have a reputation to uphold.

Great. Meanwhile her reputation was being dragged through the mud. Clearly a mere peasant girl's reputation was worth nothing to the likes of Prince Henri. Except that she wasn't a mere peasant, and even though she hadn't done anything, her reputation was sullied nonetheless. How would she ever go back to being a lady of house Tremaine now? Not that her stepmother would ever allow her back into that house. She might be naïve but she wasn't completely stupid.

She sighed for the hundredth time and disappeared into her room where she could shut out the strange world she had been thrown into. She was sure that she could win this bet with Prince Henri. She'd never been in love before and she doubted she was going to start with him. After all, what had he done so far? He'd attempted things that propriety dictated he should not, he'd teased her, he'd purchased her, and now he'd given her a very good reason not to fall in love with him.

But she didn't doubt for a second that he was going to at least try to win the bet. It might be a bet for her life, but to him it was just a game, a mere amusement to pass the time. Even though the stakes weren't high for him, she knew that he was the type of man who liked to win and he wasn't about the let a little thing like her life get in the way of that.

Pompous, self-centred man child.

She growled in frustration and roughly washed her face with cold water from the basin. He was playing to win, but so was she.

~

The bell in her room had been ringing on and off for the last thirty minutes. She wondered how long it would take for him to get the point that she wasn't coming. There was no part of their bet that said she couldn't avoid him, although she was aware that she was playing with fire by ignoring his summons.

Finally, the bell fell silent and Cinderella let out a small sigh of relief. Hopefully, the prince had found someone else to do his bidding. Satisfied with her victory, she put her full concentration back on mending the shirt in her lap. She knew it was his, the only work they seemed to give her was his.

Suddenly, the door bust open, slamming against the wall so hard that she flinched and jabbed herself with the needle. Standing in the doorway, with a dark look on his face, was Prince Henri.

Perhaps not the victory she had hoped for.

'You thought you could ignore my summons?' he demanded, his voice fiercer than she had ever heard it.

Cinderella shuddered and for the first time, she was afraid of him. Was he really so cross that she had ignored him? Had she misjudged him somehow? It wouldn't be surprising, really, she'd knew nothing about this man.

He slammed the door shut and she flinched again. He stalked towards her and for every step her took, Cinderella took one backward until she felt the cold stones at her back. Henri grabbed her wrists in his hands and pinned her to the wall, his eyes flashing with anger and desire. Her body trembled beneath him.

He looked down on her and let out a frustrated sigh. She was relieved to see his features soften slightly. His gaze flicked to her bleeding finger and he clicked his tongue, though Cinderella wasn't sure if his annoyance was directed at her or at himself.

'You should be more careful,' he said, then he brought her finger to his lips and began to suck at the wound.

Cinderella gasped and pulled against him but she could not free herself. The more she moved, the more he seemed to be enjoying himself. Finally, he put her hand back to the wall, holding it firmly in place. He leaned in, his warm breath caressing her skin. He was only inches from her face. Her heart raced in her chest and her eyes dropped to his lips before she could stop them.

'Have you fallen for me already?' he asked, his voice husky.

Cinderella met his gaze again. 'No,' she said, her own voice was breathy. It didn't sound like hers.

A smile played on his lips and he closed the distance between them, slowly, slowly inching closer. Cinderella closed her eyes, waiting for the brush of his lips on hers. But it never came. She opened her eyes to find him watching her. Her cheeks flushed with embarrassment and she averted her gaze. What was she thinking? She wanted the ground to open up and swallow her.

'That's not a bad look on you,' he said, thoroughly enjoying teasing her.

Cinderella felt the irritation bubble within her again and she lifted her head to give him a piece of her mind, but he sealed her lips with his. He kissed her roughly, passionately and her mind went blank. His tongue pushed past her lips, gently gliding along her own. The heat of his body seeped into hers, his scent enveloped her, making her lightheaded, making her forget that she was supposed to resist him.

When he pulled away, she had forgotten what she was going to say, whatever argument she had with him seemed far away. Her breathing was ragged to her own ears, her heart thumped in her chest, and that warmth in her core was now a searing heat begging for more.

She needed to get a hold of herself. She needed to snap out of this.

After a long moment, he released his grip on her and slowly pushed away. Without a word he headed for the door and Cinderella found herself wishing he would say something, wishing he would stay.

He paused in the doorway. 'Next time I call, you come,' he said, then he left without turning to look back at her, clearly unaffected by the kiss they had shared.

Cinderella was surprised at the stinging sensation in her chest. She had to snap out of this. This was merely a game to him, and he wouldn't care if he broke her heart into a thousand tiny pieces. She had to stay focused. She had to resist.

Her freedom depended on it.

CHAPTER 7

Henri

After breakfast the next morning, Henri decided to go to Cinderella. She'd snuck out on him again and he was contemplating tying her to the bed to ensure she stayed until he dismissed her. But he supposed the day she stayed would be the day he knew he'd won the bet.

He smiled at the thought of waking up with her in his arms, at the thought of her admitting that he'd won.

He strode through the servants' quarters, not minding the stares from the staff. They weren't used to seeing him in their part of the palace. He wasn't actually sure he'd been there since he was a child and now twice in as many days he'd gone to fetch Cinderella. He wondered what rumours they would concoct, the petty gossip of servants was often the most entertaining kind.

'Your highness,' Madam Dubois said hastily with a low curtsey. 'Did Cinderella not answer when you summoned? I will have her punished immediately.'

'No need. I didn't summon her,' Henri said.

Madam Dubois looked at him like he'd grown a second head before she remembered herself and quickly schooled her expression. 'Then why…?'

'Do I need a reason to move around my own palace, Madam Dubois?'

'No, of course not,' she answered quickly, curtseying low again.

'Good, carry on,' he said dismissively.

In the corner of the room, he caught sight of one of his previous girls. What was her name again? Briana? Brittany? It didn't matter. Her mouth was hanging open in shock and when she realised he was looking at her, her cheeks blushed a light shade of pink and she curtseyed lowed enough to present her cleavage to him.

Bethany. He remembered now. He'd let her go about six months back because she had become far too attached. He didn't realise she was still in the palace.

'My lord? Why didn't you ring for me?' Cinderella's voice pulled him out of his thoughts and he smiled up at her before he even realised he was doing it.

'I thought we might walk in the garden,' he said,

offering his hand.

A plate shattered on the floor and all eyes turned to the source of the sound. Bethany stood stock still, as if she'd been frozen in place, her knuckles white from the force of her grip on the tea towel, shattered ceramic at her feet.

'Foolish girl!' Madam Dubois began scolding the poor creature and everyone seemed to snap out of their trance.

Henri turned his attention back to Cinderella. 'Shall we?' he asked, his hand still hovering in the air.

Cinderella's eyes darted around as if she wasn't sure what to do, everyone was watching her now. Would she dare defy him in front of all these people? Brazen woman. He had to supress his urge to smile again. He looked at his hand then back at her, urging her to take it, almost a silent command. Almost.

Finally, she took his hand, not because she wanted to but because she felt she must. He could tell by the way she ducked her head and couldn't bring herself to meet the eyes of anyone in the room. Was that blush on her cheeks embarrassment because she had to do it or because she wanted to? Maybe both. Or perhaps that was just wishful thinking.

He led her out into the gardens, enjoying the way her eyes looked everywhere but at him. She really was an open book, and he liked that about her, there was no malice behind her actions, no scheming or plotting for things she coveted, there was a simple honesty about her, a simple goodness that he found more appealing than he had ever imagined he would.

That sense of familiarity niggled at the back of his mind but he couldn't place it. The curiosity was becoming unbearable.

'I have a question for you that you may find strange,' he said, finally bringing her attention to him.

'Because the rest of our acquaintance has been so normal?' she said, that inner fire making itself known once more. He wondered why she felt the need to hide it, but another part of him was glad that he was the only one who got to see it.

'Have we met somewhere before?'

She stopped suddenly, her eyes widening in surprise. Her reaction told him all he needed to know; they had met before. So why couldn't he remember her?

'Where?'

She looked away again and kept her mouth shut as they walked. He pulled her to a stop, forcing her to look at him. 'Where?' he asked again.

'It was a long time ago,' she said.

He pulled her closer, surprised at how little she resisted him. He placed his finger under her chin tilting her head up, and he gazed down at her, thinking that he may find the answers he sought somewhere in those piercing blue eyes, but instead the urge to kiss her lips drowned everything else out.

'Are you denying your prince?' he asked, his voice

low and rough.

'If it was important to you, then you will remember on your own,' she said, a touch of sadness in her voice. Was the memory important to her? Had it once meant something to him? It was infuriating not knowing, infuriating that she wouldn't tell him and let him take the easiest path. But perhaps her request wasn't unreasonable, he really had no way of knowing until he remembered.

What if he never remembered?

'You are infuriating when you want to be,' he said.

'It's not good for man to always get what he wants, especially when he is a prince.'

His brow furrowed as he looked down at her. 'My mother used to say that. How did you know?'

'I told you, if it's important to you, you will remember on your own.'

Impatience and frustration stirred inside him. He wanted to get the answers from her but the sound of a carriage approaching forced him to let go of his questions, to let go of Cinderella, even as every instinct in him wanted to draw her close. If he rocked the boat too much, she would be sent away.

'You may head back inside,' Henri said. 'I will call for you later.' He ran his fingers lightly across her jaw, enjoying the blush that rose to her cheeks. She bobbed a quick curtsey before hurrying away, pressing a hand to her burning cheek.

William exited the carriage and spotted his friend

immediately, offering a wave and his usual smile before walking over, completely oblivious to the fact that he had interrupted something.

'Well, that looked cosy,' William said. 'You seem to be getting along quite well with the new girl.'

Not oblivious. He knew exactly what he had interrupted. Henri let out an exasperated sigh. 'What you interrupted was an interrogation.'

'Didn't look like an interrogation. It looked like –'

'Don't finish that sentence,' Henri interrupted. God, he was getting too close, getting in too deep. Even though he could see it coming, he couldn't seem to stop running towards it. But he wasn't interested in William analysing it. He was definitely not ready for that.

'Are you pulling rank?'

'Yes.'

'Oh, this is more serious than I thought.'

Henri rolled his eyes and let out a frustrated groan.

'What information were you trying to get from her?'

'It doesn't matter. Let's just go and play darts. I'm in the mood to kick your arse now.'

'I might win today,' William protested as the pair made their way into the palace.

CHAPTER 8

Cinderella

Cinderella didn't really know why she was being so stubborn about keeping their previous meeting a secret. Some part of her told her it was logical, that if he knew then he would know that she was nobility and that would cause problems for her. But another part of her wanted him to remember her, wanted him to remember on his own, wanted to know that it was important to him, that she hadn't been a total fool.

More than anything, Cinderella wished she knew what was going on inside his head. His games, his little touches were keeping her in constant turmoil. She repeatedly caught herself thinking of his kiss, touching her fingers to her lips as though she could still feel him there.

As she entered the kitchens, Bethany slammed against her shoulder, causing Cinderella to stumble. Bethany's hatred never seemed to let up, each day it only grew stronger and Cinderella was starting to fear what outlets that hatred might start to take. She'd done her best to avoid the woman but Bethany always seemed to find her.

'You think you're so special, don't you?' she sneered. 'You think you're better than me because the prince is fawning all over you. Enjoy it while it lasts, he will get bored of you before long.'

'The same way he grew bored of you?' Cinderella asked before she could stop herself.

Bethany glared at her, malice in her eyes. Thankfully, Madam Dubois chose that moment to enter the room.

'Bethany, what have I told you? Leave the girl alone,' she snapped, sending the woman hurrying away. 'If you keep letting her bully you, it will only escalate.'

'I'll not stoop to her level,' Cinderella said.

'Then you'd best watch your back,' Madam Dubois said before she, too, went about her business.

Cinderella headed back to her room to finish her mending, locking the door behind her to ensure Bethany would not follow her inside. Madam Dubois was right about one thing, something needed to be done about Bethany before the vicious woman did something to escalate her bullying. But what was she supposed to do?

She sighed again and focused on her sewing, waiting for the bell to ring. She was starting to hate the sound less, in fact, she found herself almost looking forward to the sound each night. Henri, though shockingly inappropriate most of the time, had stayed true to his word. He had not done anything that she didn't want, not really. She hadn't wanted to share his bed each evening, but she was able to sleep now, and it wasn't a bad feeling, having his arms around her.

No. She couldn't think like that. Her freedom depended on it. Maybe she didn't want to be away from him, but she didn't want to be a slave her whole life. If slavery was the price of being close to him, she wasn't sure it was a price she was willing to pay.

The bell rang and Cinderella put aside her work, brushing the wrinkles out of her dress before heading to Henri's room.

'Come in,' Prince Henri said in response to her timid knock. She couldn't seem to bring herself to be confident when she went there. It still felt like something she should be ashamed of, even though they hadn't done anything wrong.

Cinderella gasped when she entered the room. She didn't know quite where to look, but she knew it needed to be anywhere but at Prince Henri. Why had he called her to his room while he was bathing?

Henri chuckled, watching her flustered reaction. 'Come here, Cinderella,' he ordered, his voice smooth as velvet.

'What? You can't be serious,' Cinderella said incredulously.

'There's no need for you to be shy,' he said, knowing exactly what he was doing. 'You still need to do your job while you're here. Didn't I warn you already about disobeying me?'

'You warned me against ignoring you, not disobeying you,' Cinderella said, desperately trying to find a loophole.

'If you do not come to me, then I will come to you,' Prince Henri said as though either scenario suited him just fine.

But he was definitely naked in that bathtub. Cinderella was acutely aware of that. Her cheeks flushed at the idea of him standing and coming to her with water dripping down his muscular body.

'I-I'm coming,' she said, shaking the thoughts from her mind. She slowly made her way over to the bath, careful to avert her gaze.

'Look at me,' Prince Henri said, his low voice sending a shiver through her body.

'No,' she said, her voice smaller than she had meant it to be.

'Are you disobeying me again?' he asked. When Cinderella didn't answer, he quickly stood up and grabbed her, pulling her into the warm bath water with him.

'What are you doing?!' she demanded. She wriggled

in his grasp but it was clear she was losing the battle. The water soaked into her dress, the fabric sticking to her skin.

'I told you there would be consequences,' Prince Henri said, his voice coated in satisfaction.

'You most certainly did not!' Cinderella said indignantly.

'Shhh,' Prince Henri said, the sound surprisingly sensual. Cinderella stopped struggling as his lips pressed against the nape of her neck. Her mind went blank. He gently sunk his teeth into her skin and a moan escaped her lips.

With expert fingers, he began unlacing her dress and she didn't have the presence of mind to stop him. No, it was more than that. She didn't want to stop him. He pulled the wet fabric away from her body, exposing her bare skin on her shoulders, her chest, her breasts. She could feel him growing firm against her back.

His hands slid over her wet skin, pausing at her breasts. He massaged them and growled with desire as she moaned. No one had ever touched her like that before and she found herself leaning back against him, her nipples hardening at his touch, a tingling sensation building between her legs. She could feel her letting go, losing herself to him. His lips trailed down her neck as he squeezed her nipples. She gasped, her back arching against him. She knew she shouldn't but she wanted more, she wanted to feel him on every inch of her.

He ran his hand slowly down her body, the anticipation was building in the pit of her stomach, her muscles clenching impatiently. 'Henri,' she gasped, her modesty abandoned.

Something animalistic seemed to take over him when she said his name. A growl rumbled in his chest and he took her earlobe between his teeth as his hand slipped between her thighs.

'Ah!' she moaned as he stroked her clitoris. She gripped his arm, digging her fingers into his flesh, her eyes fluttering closed.

He pulled her firmly against him, as though he could not have her close enough. His fingers continued to stroke her, to circle her sensitive bud, his other hand cupping her breast. He slid one finger inside her and she stiffened for a moment before melting into him. The pressure was becoming unbearable as she writhed against him. She cried out as her body quivered in ecstasy. Henri growled in her ear, continuing to stroke her until she finally stilled.

She relaxed against him, and he tucked a strand of her hair behind her ear. Part of her wished they could stay like this forever.

Cinderella's senses began to return to her. What had she just done? Her body stiffened awkwardly in indecision. She didn't know what to do. Should she get up? Should she stay? No. She definitely needed to leave. Would he let her?

'The water is getting cold, don't you think?' Prince

Henri asked, surprising her by coming to her rescue.

'Y-yes,' Cinderella said awkwardly. She stood up, refusing to look at him, her cheeks flushed.

She could feel his gaze on her as the water dripped down the contours of her body. She wrapped her arms around her bare chest. Getting the sodden dress back on was going to be a near impossible task but what other choice did she have?

She stiffened when she heard him get out of the water. He handed her a towel and she gratefully took it without looking at him, wrapping it around her. How was she ever supposed to look at him again?

He silently handed her some dry clothes and she felt his gaze linger on her for a long moment before he walked across the room, giving her some privacy to dress. She was surprised that he didn't' insist on watching, maybe he was more sensitive than she'd given him credit for.

She quickly dressed, afraid that at any moment he would turn around, but he kept his back to her until she was fully clothed.

'You can leave,' he said, the words a little colder than she'd expected.

'What?' she asked, her confusion showing in her tone. He would really do all that to her and tell her to leave? Why was she feeling so hurt? Wasn't that what she had hoped for?

A wicked smile sprung to his lips. 'Unless you'd prefer to stay?' he asked.

Cinderella swallowed hard. Part of her did want to stay, but she knew it would be dangerous if she did. She'd already let him…her cheeks flared red and she looked at her feet. 'Good night, my lord,' she said and with an awkward curtsey, she escaped back to her room.

CHAPTER 9

Henri

Henri couldn't help feeling disappointed. It stung at him even though night had turned to day. He'd given her the choice to stay or to leave but she had chosen to leave. After two weeks of working on her, really trying to get her to fall for him, she stubbornly refused to open her heart to him.

Why?

Well, that was a stupid question. He'd gone and dangled her freedom in front of her as if she would never have the option in the future. Which, now that he thought about it, she might not. He'd always gotten bored of the women sooner or later and they'd leave with enough money to set them up nicely, or they stayed and worked at the palace for a wage, but with Cinderella, he felt as though he would never tire of her, as though he never wanted to set her free.

He should have offered something else. Something less appealing.

The dart sailed through the air and sunk into the wood next to the board. Henri hardly noticed as he lined up the next one, his body going through the motions as his mind whirled. He was very much in danger of falling in love with Cinderella, how could she remain so unaffected?

'Okay, what is going on?' William said.

'What?'

'Much as I want to win, it's no fun if you're not here for me to gloat. Is it your new girl?'

Always so perceptive. Sometimes Henri forgot he wore the disguise of fool draped over a fierce intelligence. 'No,' he lied. He wasn't ready for William to know all the details of his…whatever this was with Cinderella. Maybe he could pretend it was something else bothering him. The ball, maybe? Or…

'What, did she reject you or something?' he scoffed, cutting off Henri's train of thought, but when Henri didn't say anything, his eyes grew wide. 'She rejected you?'

William's laughter made Henri grind his teeth. 'Laugh it up.'

She didn't really reject him. Okay, maybe she did sort of. She was probably just embarrassed, ashamed of what she'd let him do to her, she needed time to process. Or maybe he should have reassured her? Well, he couldn't do that now with William about.

When did he get so dense?

'I'm sorry,' William said, wiping invisible tears from his eyes, 'I'm sorry. It's just, well, it's about time someone did.'

'She's only doing it to win the bet,' Henri said, though his voice sounded sulky even to his own ears. The dumbest bet he had ever made.

'Bet? Do tell.' He'd peaked William's curiosity. Damn it.

'I bet her that if she didn't fall in love with me in a month, I'd grant her freedom.'

William's brow furrowed. 'You would have done that anyway, that's what you do.'

'She didn't know that.' Henri was actually surprised that none of the other staff had told her as much. Madam Dubois' doing, no doubt.

'And what would you get?'

'Same thing I already have. She'd be mine until I said otherwise.'

'So why make the bet?' He could see the wheels in William's head turning as he began to formulate some theory or other.

'I thought it would be amusing,' Henri snapped, sending another dart sailing through the air with more force than necessary, its tip sinking deep into the wood next to the dart board.

'Oh shit, you're in love with her.'

Henri stilled for a moment before he responded, 'I

am not.' It was like the man could see through him. Was he being that obvious? He'd need to work on that.

'Uh-huh. Well, it's good that you aren't since she's a slave and you could never marry her and you've got that whole ball thing coming up in a couple of weeks.'

Why did he have to put everything into perspective like that? He didn't care about the damn ball, he wasn't planning on choosing a wife, and William was right, there was no way his father would allow him to marry a slave, or even a servant.

'You're a bastard, you know that?' Henri said.

'You could always keep her as your mistress. I'm sure your wife would love that,' William said with a shrug.

Henri glared at him.

'All I'm saying is that you have a position to think of. Unless she turns into a noble lady at the stroke of midnight, which I believe is unlikely, maybe it would be kinder if you just let her go, rather than setting her up for heartache.'

There it was, the point William was coming to. He was being a selfish prick, trying to make Cinderella fall in love with him when all that would mean for her is heartbreak. He couldn't marry her, couldn't give her the life she dreamed of. He could keep her as a mistress, but that would never make her happy. It wouldn't matter how much he loved her, she'd be his dirty little secret for the rest of her life, as would any children they might have.

He didn't want that for her.

But how could he stop? Selfish as ever, he wanted everything. If he could hold off on marrying until after he became king, could he marry who he wanted then? Would she even wait that long for him? Could he ask her to?

'I hate you.'

'I know,' William said with a smile. 'It's not an easy job, but someone has to make you think about other people every now and then.'

'I need a drink,' Henri said.

'An excellent choice. Let's go and drown your sorrows,' William agreed, and the two of them rang for a servant.

Henri wasn't sure that hard liquor would actually keep him from thinking of Cinderella, but he had to do something to occupy William. Whatever else happened that afternoon, he'd definitely had enough of his friend's annoyingly accurate advice. He wasn't ready to give up on this yet, he would try to find a way to keep her.

CHAPTER 10

Cinderella

Cinderella stayed in her room until her stomach grumbled so loudly she couldn't ignore it anymore. It was midday when she finally emerged. For the first time since she had arrived, she felt like everyone knew what she had done, she felt ashamed of her actions. It was different before, when their speculations were unfounded.

If it was so shameful, why had she let him do it? It certainly felt good, better than she'd ever known it could be. As her memory turned back to his touch, her cheeks blushed again and her muscles clenched in want.

What was he doing to her?

'I thought you were going to hide in your room forever,' Bethany's cold voice echoed lightly down the empty hallway.

Cinderella spun around to see the woman leaning against the wall as if she had been laying in wait all day. She swallowed, the look in Bethany's eye was dark and unnatural. 'What are you doing here?' she asked, hoping that if she put enough confidence in her voice, Bethany would lose interest.

'You think I enjoy waiting for you?' she sneered. 'I know what you did last night. You're not as good as you pretend. Did if feel good to have the prince inside you knowing that he was inside me first?'

The thought of Henri being intimate with this vile woman made her sick to her stomach. She forced herself to stand her ground. 'Your jealousy is showing, you might want to fix that.'

'So superior,' Bethany said with a shake of her head. 'Let's see what we can do about that.' She shoved Cinderella to the ground and pinned her there, face down on the stone floor, positioning herself on top of her so she couldn't move.

'Get off!' Cinderella protested as she tried to break free.

Bethany gathered her hair and pulled it hard until Cinderella cried out in pain. 'Let's see how much he likes you now,' she hissed.

The sound of the scissors cutting through her hair made Cinderella still, tears pricking at her eyes, and she sunk her teeth into her lip. She wouldn't cry. She wouldn't give Bethany that satisfaction.

The woman finally released her, standing and brushing the wrinkles from her dress. Cinderella jumped to her feet, her vision beginning to blur. All she could do was watch as Bethany walked away, leaving her to stand alone with her own hair strewn across the floor around her.

With a shaking hand she reached up and ran her fingers through what was left of her hair. She went back into her room and shut the door firmly behind her, her hunger forgotten. She curled up on the bed and let her tears flow as she hugged her knees to her chest.

What had she done to deserve this? What had she done that was so bad she wasn't allowed a moment of happiness?

She found herself wishing for her mother. If only she had lived, her life would have been so different.

She didn't know how long she stayed like that but the tears had stopped on their own, as if she had run out of tears to cry. Her mind felt numb. If she managed to actually win the bet with the prince, she wasn't sure she'd make it out alive. Would they fire someone to protect a mere slave? If they did fire her, she'd just be waiting for the day Cinderella left the palace and there would be no one to protect her out there.

The door slammed open and Cinderella flinched as she looked up, half expecting Bethany to be standing in the doorway, but instead, it was Henri with a cross look on his face. She had been so lost in her own head that she hadn't even heard the bell ring.

'I thought I made it clear that there were consequences to disob –' he began but stopped as he took in the sight of her. God, she must look a mess. She quickly wiped her face with her hand and reached for her hair but stopped when she remembered that most of it was now gone. She turned away from him, hoping to keep some tiny amount of dignity.

Henri knelt before her, turning her face to him with a gentler touch than she had ever known from him. 'Who did this?' he asked.

Though he tried to keep his emotions under control, Cinderella could sense the fury behind those words. Should she tell him? What would happen to Bethany if she did? What would happen to her?

'Cinderella, who did this?' he asked again as his thumb caressed her cheek. His eyes were full of concern and her heart ached. She was losing the bet, she could feel it, she could feel her heart opening to him even though she knew better.

'Bethany,' she said, her voice quiet and shaky.

Henri pulled her into his arms, wrapping them protectively around her and she was surprised to find that she actually felt safe there. But how long would that last? How long could he protect her? How long until he really did grow bored of her and move on to the next one?

As if he could hear her thoughts, his arms tightened

around her. He didn't know how cruel he was being, did he? He didn't realise what he was asking of her. She felt tears prick at her eyes again and she buried her face in his chest.

She wanted to ask him what he was thinking, she wanted to ask him if this was still just a game to him, she wanted to ask him so many things but she was afraid to know the answers to those questions, afraid to hear the things she didn't want to hear.

Maybe it was okay to have this, just for now. Maybe it was okay to have him, just for now.

CHAPTER 11

Henri

Henri held Cinderella in his arms until she fell asleep, a silent fury building in his chest. Not only because someone had dared to hurt her, destroy what belonged to him, but because it was in part his fault.

An example had to be made.

After that, he would call a barber to fix her hair. It would grow back in time, but it needn't be a hacked mess until that point. Then he would have to find some way to make it up to her.

He gently placed her in the bed and pulled the blanket over her. He stroked her head as he stared down at her, that familiarity niggling at his mind again. It was the short hair, had he seen her with short hair before?

He would have to think about that later, for now, he had work to do.

He kissed her head and left her alone in her room to sleep, he had no doubt she needed it. In the kitchen the staff fell silent as he entered. He wasn't surprised, they were probably talking about what had happened. Someone would have had to clean up the mess, Bethany had probably bragged about her perceived victory.

'Your highness, what brings you down to the servants' quarters?' Madam Dubois asked.

She genuinely seemed oblivious to what had transpired. 'Where is Bethany?'

Madam Dubois' eyes scanned the room and stopped on the culprit who was peeling potatoes in the corner of the room. 'Come forward, girl,' she ordered.

Bethany did as she was told. There was a nervousness about her. She curtsied low and kept her eyes on the floor.

'I hear you have a penchant for cutting hair,' Henri almost growled. The girl looked up at him in fear and Madam Dubois blinked in surprise.

'Tell me you didn't,' she hissed at Bethany.

Bethany remained silent, she may as well have announced her guilt to the room.

'Fifty lashes should be sufficient, don't you think, Madam Dubois?' Henri posed it as a question but it was an order. Unless she came back with a higher number, the order would be carried out.

'For cutting someone's hair? Please, your highness, show mercy,' Bethany pleaded.

'You have damaged something that belongs to me, something important, and you have done so maliciously. Do you really think I will show you mercy?' Henri asked darkly. 'Be thankful that I will not be carrying out your punishment personally.'

Bethany shrank before his furious gaze and Madam Dubois grabbed her by the arm, pushing her towards a chair. 'Stand there,' she said and grabbed a bamboo stick. He could see in her face that the older woman didn't enjoy this sort of thing, but it was better she did it, she didn't have Henri's strength and he didn't think he could hold back.

Bethany raised her skirt, showing her bare calves to the entire room as Madam Dubois took her place and began. Henri watched with a stony expression, his arms folded over his chest as the girl cried out with every slap of the bamboo stick across her bare skin. The skin was beginning to grow red and swell.

Madam Dubois looked at him questioningly, a hope in her eyes that he would allow her to stop.

'That's twenty-five by my count, Madam Dubois. Continue,' he said.

Bethany began to sob but she stayed where she was. Madam Dubois pulled her arm back for another strike.

'Stop!'

Suddenly, Cinderella was standing in front of

Bethany, her arms stretched out wide as she shielded the girl with her own body, even as her short hair hung around her face, a reminder of what the wretched woman had done to her only hours ago.

'Move aside, girl. This prince is doing this for you,' Madam Dubois said quietly.

'Well, I bid that he would not order such cruelty in my name,' Cinderella said boldly, looking him dead in the eye.

'Her actions require punishment,' Henri said as if that should be all the explanation Cinderella would need.

Instead of understanding, he saw stubbornness set into her features. Why was it that this woman could so boldly defend others and yet she couldn't seem to defend herself? 'I will take the remaining lashes, then.'

The room fell silent, even Bethany's sobs stopped and she looked down at the girl she had been bullying, the girl she had wronged, a look of astonishment on her face that mirrored what Henri felt.

'Why?'

'Because this is wrong.'

'Very well, if it is such a cruel punishment, I will have to come up with another. Get her out of the palace,' he said.

He saw the disappointment on Cinderella's face but he wouldn't back down from this. If she was to get out of her punishment, he would get her out of his palace. He couldn't risk that she would try something else, what if next time she did something worse, something irreparable? It wasn't a risk he was willing to take.

'You heard the prince. Come down and collect your things,' Madam Dubois said sternly and the girl did as she was told, weeping as she disappeared down the hallway.

'You come with me,' Henri said to Cinderella. He took her hand and dragged her though the palace, into his room.

'You didn't have to dismiss her,' Cinderella said as he closed the door.

He pulled her into his arms. 'Yes, I did. Who knows what she'll do next time.'

'What if she's waiting for me when I win my freedom?' Cinderella asked.

Henri couldn't quite stop the growl that rumbled in his chest. 'You're so sure that you'll win?'

After everything, her heart was still her own. After everything, she still wanted to leave him. He was running out of time and he was torn. William's words rang in his head. There had to be a way to keep her, a way for them to be happy together.

'Are you going to hold me all day?' she asked, there was a slight blush in her cheeks as she said it. Could he take that to mean she wanted him, too? She had already been subjected to a lot for one day. He would go easy on her. But just for one day.

He let her go and handed her a book. 'Read to me,' he said, then sat on the floor in front of the fireplace.

He patted the ground in front of him, indicated for her to sit. She did as he asked, the blush in her cheeks deepening as she rested her back against his chest and began to read.

CHAPTER 12

Cinderella

The other staff members had been walking on eggshells around her since Bethany was let go. Cinderella couldn't help feeling that they blamed her for it, even though she had been the victim of Bethany's vicious bullying.

With Bethany gone, there was extra work that others had to take up until a new girl could be hired. Cinderella had put her hand up in a vain attempt to get the other servants to treat her like a human being.

She regretted it almost instantly.

She stood awkwardly with the other breakfast staff in the biggest dining room she had ever seen in her life. A dining table that could sit fifty people, and yet the only ones there were the king and Prince Henri, which was probably for the best seeing as how they had argued for the entire meal so far.

'You cannot keep refusing to marry, Henri!' the king bellowed.

'Why are you so determined, father? You're not planning to kick the bucket already, are you?'

The king's face twisted in rage. 'Insolent brat!' he bellowed. 'The ball will go ahead as planned and you will choose your wife or I will choose one for you. Now, get out of my sight.'

Prince Henri stood, leaving his half-finished breakfast on the table. His eyes met with Cinderella's and he winked at her before leaving the room. Choose his wife? Something stabbed at her heart as she repeated those words over and over in her head.

Questions ran through her mind, none of them that she could answer. But part of her felt sorry for Henri. He was the most sought-after bachelor in the kingdom, but none of the women vying for his hand actually wanted him, they wanted his title and the wealth and power that went along with it. Was that the reason he acted out as he did? The reason he kept girls around for pleasure? She found herself growing more and more curious about this man who held her very future in his hands.

When she was dismissed, Cinderella set off to find Prince Henri. She ignored the strange looks the other servants were giving her as she searched the palace, but she couldn't find him anywhere. She took one final look around the garden and let out a sigh. Where could he have gotten to?

'Looking for me?' Henri's teasing voice whispered in her ear.

She spun around, startled. 'Yes, I was.'

His eyebrows jumped in surprise. 'Oh? You're being surprisingly honest today.' A triumphant smile tugged at the corner of his mouth.

Now that she had found him, she wasn't really sure what to say. It wasn't any of her business, and he seemed to be doing just fine. Would he think it was strange for her to worry about him? He should. She thought it was strange for her to worry about him.

'What are you thinking so hard about?' Henri asked. Though his words were teasing as always, his eyes were softer than Cinderella had ever seen them.

'I just wanted to see how you were doing after this morning,' Cinderella said bashfully.

'Were you worried about me?' he asked, surprise flashed across his face but it was only for a moment.

'I suppose I never considered the pressures you face because of your title.'

'That's probably because I'm singularly selfish,' Henri said and chuckled. He slipped his arm around her waist and pulled her to him. 'Shall I show you just how selfish I am?' he said softly, his husky voice sending a shiver of anticipation up her spine.

'You shouldn't do this here,' Cinderella forced the words out of her mouth. 'Someone could see.'

'And?'

She looked up, her eyes becoming trapped in his gaze. It was like nothing in the world existed to him, there was only her. Her heart hammered in her chest. The air around them felt electric and she wanted desperately for him to kiss her, for him to take her to his room. She thought of his naked body and a heat stirred in her core.

'If you keep looking at me like that, I'm going to have to break my promise to you,' Henri said, his voice rough with desire. 'Or did I win your heart already?'

Yes, her heart sighed. 'N-no. No, of course not,' she said, coming back to reality. He couldn't win, she couldn't let that happen. If she did, what kind of life would that be? He would have to choose a wife soon, and he was never going to choose her.

Something sad flashed in his eyes but it was gone too quickly for her to discern what it meant. It seemed to Cinderella that fate was a cruel mistress. By all rights, she should have been a perfectly acceptable candidate for Henri to choose, she was a lady of house Tremaine, after all, or at least she had been. But a prince could never marry a slave.

A bittersweet smile touched her lips. 'Things could have been so different.' The words slipped off her tongue before she could catch them. She risked looking up at Henri; his eyes held a silent question. Perhaps he was thinking about it too, about their difference in status. Was it too conceited to hope that he felt something for her?

'Prince Henri?' A voice called out, shattering the moment like glass.

Henri reluctantly moved away from her before they could be seen and she watched as he disappeared back into the palace.

There was only one way for her to protect herself now. She couldn't stay and watch him marry someone else.

He had won their bet.

CHAPTER 13

Henri

Henri's mother had finally succumbed to her illness. That's what the doctors said when she died in the night. If his father thought he was handling it well, he was delusional. He'd shut down, it was as if he was empty inside now that his wife was gone.

Henri's birthday had only been two days after but there had been no celebration, for which he was glad. But his father hadn't come to see him, hadn't left his room since she passed. Now that they were burying her, Henri couldn't bear to watch.

He'd snuck away in the crowd and disappeared between the headstones. He sat under a tree and wanted to cry but he couldn't seem to shed a tear. He wondered if his mother would be sad that he couldn't even cry at her funeral, would she be disappointed in him?

'Who are you visiting?' a soft voice interrupted his thoughts.

He looked up to see a young girl staring at him, kindness and sadness in her eyes, but her sadness was her own and nothing to do with him. She was the first person in weeks who had looked at her as if he were not some piteous creature. She had short blonde hair and bright blue eyes, and there was a softness about her, the kind you see in people who are raised to be good, who have never really known hardship, though what would he know about hardship, really?

'I'm not visiting.'

She looked behind him and noticed the funeral in progress. 'You're here for the queen? I'm supposed to be over there too but...' she trailed off and sat beside him as if they had known each other a long time. 'My father doesn't like to come here, he misses mama too much. I wanted to talk to her while we were here.'

'Your mother died, too?'

'The queen is your mother?' she asked astonished and he nodded solemnly. 'I'm sorry.' She took his hand then, winding her fingers through his. No one had ever done anything so bold before. She ran her thumb over the back of his hand in little circles. 'My mama used to do this when I was sad. It always made me feel better.'

'You know I'm the prince, right?'

'Obviously,' she said and for the first time in weeks, he smiled. 'Better?'

His brow furrowed for a moment as he realised that her little gesture was, in fact, comforting him. 'What's your name?'

'I'm Cinderella of house Tremaine.'

'Prince Henri!' voices called, guards and servants looking for

him, finally realising that he had gone.

'I'd better go,' he said, taking his hand from hers. He stood and brushed the grass off his pants.

'Will I see you again?' she asked. They were the very words he had been thinking.

He smiled at her. 'Obviously. I'm going to marry you one day.'

Henri woke with a smile on his face. How could he have forgotten the girl from the cemetery? He looked at the empty space beside him and sighed again. Yet again she had snuck away in the night.

Wait.

House Tremaine? Cinderella was nobility. But how did she come to be a slave? Madam Dubois wouldn't have bought her if she'd known. What had happened to that innocent girl who had never known hardship? She certainly knew it now.

Anger burned in his veins.

Whoever did this to her was going to pay dearly.

But first he wanted to tell Cinderella that he remembered her. And tell her he planned to keep that promise he'd made as a child, because now that he knew who she was, there was nothing to stop him from keeping it.

He threw his clothes on and raced to the servants' quarters. He burst into her room and froze. She wasn't there but on the ground was a single shoe, as if she had left in such a hurry that she hadn't turned back for it.

But why?

A sinking feeling crept into his chest.

Though he looked for her through the entire palace, there was no sign of Cinderella. She was gone.

He sent an urgent message to William and waited, impatiently pacing in the gardens outside. What the bloody hell was taking so long?

Finally, William galloped up the drive on horseback, his appearance more dishevelled than it normally would be. He jumped off and strode towards Henri, concern in his face slowly fading as he noticed the prince seemed unharmed.

'You said it was an emergency. What the devil is going on?'

'She's gone.'

'Who?'

'Cinderella. She ran away in the night,' Henri snapped.

Why had she run away? Right when he remembered, right when he realised that the impossible was very possible, and the future he longed for was in his grasp, she'd chosen that moment to run. What if he never found her again?

'Maybe that's for the best,' William said, doing his best to offer a comforting smile as he delivered his devastating blow.

'No, it bloody isn't. Do you remember the girl I told you about from the cemetery when I was a child?'

'From house Tremaine? Sure. Hey, why don't you marry her?' William asked, not grasping the hint Henri had thrown at him. Henri raised an eyebrow. 'What?'

'That was Cinderella.'

William stared dumbfoundedly at his friend for a long moment. 'No. How?'

'Well, I wanted to ask her that except she vanished. Now, help me find her,' Henri said.

'Where are we supposed to start? She could be anywhere,' William said.

'We'll start at her home and work our way through the kingdom until we find her,' Henri growled. He grabbed his horse from the stables and the two of them mounted. William looked like he wanted to say something and Henri was grateful that he'd kept his mouth shut. He spurred his horse forward. The only thing that mattered now was finding Cinderella, and when he did, he'd make sure she never got away from him again.

CHAPTER 14

Cinderella

Cinderella knew when her window of opportunity would be, knew the only chance she had of escaping was while Henri slept. She'd snuck out of his bed many times now, though it had always been early morning. This time, she had to do it as soon as possible to give her enough time to put some distance between her and the palace.

Henri's breathing began to deepen, to relax, his body grew heavy as it let go of consciousness. Cinderella waited there, his arms around her, the warmth of his body willing her to stay. And oh how she wanted to stay, to close her eyes and fall asleep with him, to tell him he'd won the bet and be with him for as long as he would allow.

But how long could that last?

Maybe she should just tell her that she was nobility, but even if she did, he'd never expressed a wish to marry her, he'd never said he loved her or let on that she was special, different to the others he'd had before. Maybe he felt he couldn't because he knew that it wouldn't change the inevitable.

The ball was less than a week away now. Henri would have to choose a wife and it wasn't going to be her. She couldn't stay and watch the man she loved marry someone else.

This had turned out to be a crueller game than she had ever imagined.

Cinderella took a deep breath to still her emotions, to calm her nerves and steel her resolve. This was the only option she had now. She would be a runaway slave, a fugitive, she would never be able to go home, not that it had felt like home in a long time. But she would be free and she could try to have a good life.

She slipped out of the bed, Henri groaned in his sleep, his arm reached out for her but he stilled when she pulled the covers over him. 'Goodbye,' she whispered, her voice barely audible in the silence of the room.

The clock had started ticking now.

Cinderella ran down the hallway, through the kitchen and dug through the little box where the cook kept a little money. One day, when she was earning her own money, she would return it. She hoped that for now, he would understand.

My Sweet Cinderella

She darted into her room and grabbed her coat. As she dashed through the door, her shoe slipped off her foot. She made to go back for it but a voice startled her.

Someone was awake.

She quickly fled from the palace, leaving the shoe behind. The cold ground bit into her bare foot as she ran through the grounds. As she came to the gate, she slowed her pace. There was only one way out of the palace and it was guarded. But everyone in the palace knew her role and if she could only lie well enough, it would be over.

'Where are you going so late at night?'

'I'm...not supposed to say,' Cinderella said, looking around as if someone might be watching.

'You're the prince's little plaything, aren't you?'

Cinderella nodded. 'Please, I'm only doing as his highness instructed.'

'Not running away?' he asked, his scrutinising gaze raking over her and she hid her bare foot behind her leg.

'Where would I run to? Besides, I'm treated far better here than I would be anywhere else,' she said.

The guard nodded in agreement. 'Alright, but hurry back, my shift ends at dawn and if you're not back by then you'll have a time getting back in.'

Cinderella nodded, smiling gratefully at the guard. It didn't matter if it was difficult to get back in or not, she wasn't coming back.

She walked through the gates, along the drive, until finally the guard was out of sight and then she sprinted into the darkness. Henri could wake at any moment and then the chase would begin.

Or maybe it wouldn't.

Maybe he would simply wake to find her gone, shrug his shoulders and find another girl to take her place.

Tears pricked at her eyes and she forced them back. She couldn't keep torturing herself like this. He'd crept into her mind, into her heart and scrambled everything about like a child playing in the mud. Nothing made sense anymore. Did his little touches mean anything? Was he protective because he loved her or simply because he didn't like others touching what belonged to him?

She wiped away an errant tear as it slid down her cheek and a crack of lightning split the sky. A moment later, rain began to fall and she ran for shelter in the darkened streets. Finally, she came upon a building with light shining through the windows, a tavern. She pushed open the door and hoped that the money she'd taken was enough to give her a room for the night. If she could only have some place dry and warm to rest and think for a day or two, she could come up with some kind of plan.

'Good heavens, girl, look at the state of you,' the man behind the counter said as he looked her over. He was an aging man with a kindly face but she wondered if he would kick her out, if she looked like a beggar who had wandered in off the streets.

Cinderella couldn't help blushing as she looked down at herself, feeling ashamed of her bedraggled appearance, mud coating her feet, clothes and hair soaked from the rain. Little puddles of water began to pool around her and she felt guilty for making such a mess.

'I'm sorry for making a mess, only I –'

'None of that. Helen!' he called over his shoulder then smiled warmly at Cinderella. 'We'll get you cleaned up and Helen will lend you something to wear.'

Cinderella blinked in surprise. 'I couldn't ask you to go to all that trouble.'

'You didn't ask, I'm offering, and I won't take no for an answer.'

A woman appeared at his side, silver strands of hair weaved through her dark locks. She had the same kindness about her as the bartender. 'Goodness,' she said, looking at Cinderella in shock. 'You'd better come with me before you catch your death.'

She led Cinderella up the stairs to a room, lit a fire and told her she'd be back with some towels and some clothes. As soon as the door shut, Cinderella sobbed, sinking to the floor in front of the fireplace. It was as if the kindness of the couple had pulled open the bottle she had been trying so hard to keep closed.

What was she going to do now?

Days had passed and Cinderella was growing accustomed to her new life with relative ease. Helen and George, the bartender, had offered her a job, which she had accepted. It didn't pay much but she had a place to sleep and she was fed, and she found she liked the couple very much.

The patrons at the tavern were mostly a good sort, hard working men who drank there a lot. She wondered if it was really so easy, if she could just stay there and be content. She'd fallen from nobility to a bar wench, but she felt more accepted in that bar than she had since her parents died.

From time to time, she found herself thinking about Henri. Wondering what he was doing, if he missed her, if he was okay. Alright, she thought about him almost constantly, even as she tried not to.

'It's never been so busy at the shop, thanks to that ball!' the tailor remarked gleefully as she served another round of drinks to the patrons. Then he swigged his fresh beer as if he had earned it, which he probably had. The ball meant that a lot of the businesses were incredibly busy in preparation.

'Are you sure you should be here drinking then? It's tomorrow night, after all,' one of the other men said.

'Bah! There's always time for a drink, lads!' the

tailor said and was met with roars of laughter from his comrades.

'I heard a rumour that the prince has been searching the kingdom for a woman,' said one of the men.

'Wha?' said another in disbelief. 'Come off it.'

'It's true! They say she slipped through his fingers and he's desperate to find her.'

Cinderella's heart jumped to her throat. Could he really be looking for her? Was it to punish her for running away or could she dare hope that he returned her feelings? If he was desperate, surely it was the latter.

'Oh, aye, I bet she slipped right through his fingers,' the man said and the tavern filled with laughter once more.

'I think you heard wrong, Bill,' another agreed.

Of course, he'd heard wrong. What was she thinking? Why would he be looking for a slave? He might, though. He might be angry that she'd left without his permission, that she'd left before the bet was completed. If that was the reason he was looking for her, she hoped he never found her. It would be best for both of them.

Cinderella went down to the cellar to fetch another keg of beer, the customers were going through it at an alarming rate as they celebrated their good fortune. She was surprised none of them had been sick yet. She could hear the men cheerfully chatting away upstairs and she smiled to herself. It was nice to be around that kind of merriment, her world had seemed bleak for a while now, perhaps their joy would rub off on her.

Suddenly, silence fell upon the room. Wondering what could have possibly happened to garner such a reaction from the highly intoxicated patrons, Cinderella hurried back up with the keg.

She instantly wished that she had not.

Prince Henri was standing at the bar, handing some gold coins to George. He looked tired, like he hadn't slept in days. His usual confidence seemed to be drained form him, and his shoulders drooped ever so slightly.

Cinderella's breath hitched in her throat and she dropped the keg of beer to the ground with a loud thud. Henri's head snapped up and his eyes locked onto her. There was a silent fury in those eyes, a raging storm of emotions and she gulped nervously.

She supposed she would finally find out why he had been searching for her now. What scared her most was that if he took her back, she didn't know if she had the strength to resist her feelings anymore.

What kind of life would that mean for her?

CHAPTER 15

Henri

Henri had been searching for days now and there was no sign of Cinderella. At William's suggestion, he had not been present when her family had been questioned. William pretended to be the prince's man servant and garnered all the sordid details. Henri was glad he hadn't been there, it would not have ended well.

To think that her own family had treated her so abominably. No wonder her freedom had been so important to her. But she was so close to getting it, why would she run away now? Unless he had won the bet. But, if she loved him, why would she leave?

Of course, he couldn't confide any of this to William, his friend would only offer sensible answers that he wasn't in the mood to hear.

'We've been looking for days now, the ball is tomorrow night. Maybe you should just give up,' William said, offering a sympathetic smile.

'No. She has to be here somewhere.'

'It's a pretty big kingdom.'

'I don't care, William.'

William sighed. 'Well, we'll have to stop for the night, what about in there?'

'Fine.'

He walked into the tavern while William stabled the horses. It was a rowdy place, until the drunkards realised who he was, then silence fell upon the tavern.

'Your highness,' the man behind the bar said and bowed awkwardly.

'I need two rooms for the night,' he said and held out the coins to the man. Probably too much but he didn't care. He didn't care about much of anything anymore.

He supposed he should ask them if they had seen Cinderella, but he'd been giving her description to people all day and getting the same response: they didn't know her, they hadn't seen her. He'd had enough disappointment for one day, he'd ask them tomorrow before they left.

A heavy thud made him look up and for a moment he didn't believe what he was seeing. Cinderella was standing before him in the dress of a humble woman that clearly didn't belong to her, it was too tight in the chest, too loose around the waist and hips. But it was definitely her. His expression turned stony.

'Mary, be careful. You'll hurt yourself,' the bartender said, his voice full of concern.

'Mary?' Henri asked, a growl in his voice.

'It was my mother's name,' Cinderella said meekly.

'Why don't you show the prince to his room,' the bartender said, clearly picking up on the fact that they had things to discuss.

Cinderella looked at the man almost pleadingly, which was infuriating. Did she really care so little? Didn't he deserve an explanation?

The bartender only smiled encouragingly at her and shooed her off. She let out a little sigh and headed for the stairs. She didn't speak to him as they walked, didn't turn to look at him. Her silence only stoked the rage in his chest. It was unbearable.

Finally, she entered a room and he slammed the door shut behind them, startling her. She finally faced him, her complexion pale as if in fear. He couldn't do anything about that now, he was too enraged to comfort her, too hurt to want to try.

'I heard a rumour,' she said finally, her voice cracking with nervousness. 'They said you were searching for someone.'

'Perhaps I was searching for an explanation,' he said, the coldness in his voice making her flinch.

'An explanation for what, my lord?' she asked. As if she didn't already know.

She had to know. Had he misjudged her? Was she

playing games with him? He ground his teeth, trying to calm his temper. 'Why did you leave? We had a deal.'

That wasn't the reason he wanted to know. The deal didn't matter to him at all. If she had won their bet, he still wouldn't have been able to let her go, he would have broken his word. Maybe she knew that, maybe she read him better than he'd ever imagined.

'Yes, we did.' She let out a sigh of defeat and then looked up at him, holding his gaze with her own, a look of determination on her face. 'I lost.'

'What?' The anger vanished, like a candle being snuffed out it was gone and what was left was confusion. Had he misheard her?

'I lost. And I couldn't bear to watch you marry someone else, so, I left.' She shrugged her shoulders and smiled self-depreciatingly. Tears began to fill her eyes. 'I guess, in the end, you were right.'

She'd lost. How could he be so blind? She'd lost the bet. She'd fallen in love with him. Henri crossed the room and pulled her into his arms. He couldn't wait a second longer. He would never let her go again.

'My lord?' she asked, surprised.

Perhaps she had been expecting something else, perhaps he hadn't shown her the depth of his own feelings. No, he definitely hadn't shown her that, if he had, maybe she would never have run away.

'Shut up,' he growled before crushing his lips hungrily to hers. She gasped at the intensity of it and he took advantage of the opening, slipping his tongue between her teeth, entwining it with hers.

God, he'd almost lost her because he hadn't shown her how he felt. He wouldn't let that happen again.

A moan escaped her and he pulled her closer, trying to eliminate any space between them. He couldn't hold back this time, if she didn't stop him, he would have her this night and every night after. His hands roamed over her dress, gripping her arse as he pressed his aching cock against her.

He tugged at the laces of her dress with impatient hands, fingers skimming across her to find the places where bare skin peeked through fabric. He'd been dreaming of this day since he'd pulled her into that bath, since he'd brought her to come on his hand. Christ, he needed to be inside her.

Her dress slipped to the floor with barely a protest and he made short work of her underclothes. All the while Cinderella looked at him like he was everything, like he was her whole world. Desire coloured her cheeks and made her breasts swell with every breath.

'If you keep looking at me like that, I'll never let you leave this bedroom,' he said.

'Good,' she responded.

He laid her down on the bed and pushed her thighs apart with his leg. Her body shuddered in anticipation as his cock brushed against her opening. He dropped his lips to her neck, her collar bone, her breasts. He took her nipple between his teeth, sucking until she cried out in pleasure. Her hand gripped the bedding as his lips travelled lower and lower. He wanted to taste every inch of her. Impatience was building but he forced himself to take this slowly. It was her first time and he wanted to make it perfect for her.

He slipped his arms behind her knees, gripping onto her hips as he pulled her to his mouth. He flicked his tongue skilfully, enjoying the way she writhed against him, the sound of her voice as she moaned. She was already getting close, he could feel it, he could see it in the way her limbs began to tremble with tension, the way her fingers curled into his hair, pushing and pulling him as if she had become so sensitive she didn't know if she wanted him to stop or continue. A wicked smile touched his lips and he pulled away from her. A whimper escaped her.

'Not yet, love,' he said softly.

He moved up her body slowly, kissing her hip, her stomach, taking a nipple briefly between his teeth and sending her crying out again, before finally hovering above her, his weight on his forearms as he smiled seductively. He pressed his lips to hers, the tip of his cock once again brushing against her entrance. Her hips wiggled as she tried to get closer, silently begging him for the thing he wanted most in that moment. He pushed himself inside her, slowly, agonisingly slowly, easing his way in so as not to hurt her. The discomfort and pleasure mixed on her face, that same expression of stop-don't-stop.

When he filled her completely, he stopped, kissing

her long and deep as he waited for her to relax around him. It felt like an eternity, the urge to fuck her pulled at him, his cock pulsed with need.

'Please!' she begged.

He needed no other encouragement.

Henri growled, pulling her against him. He pulled out and thrust deep inside her, she cried out, her fingers dug into his back as she clung to him, her teeth finding his shoulder and biting down.

He hissed as he began to rock his hips, burying his face in her neck, his breath hot in her hair. She wrapped her legs around him and pulled him closer, writhing beneath him as he moved, seeking a release from the quivering tension that had gripped her body.

His hips bucked against her, picking up speed with every moan that came from her lips. He groaned, thrust against her as finally the pressure broke and she was released in a wave of quivering pleasure, crying out his name as she clung to him.

They collapsed, limbs still entangled, both entirely exhausted, chests rising and falling heavily with every breath.

'You remember our bet?' Henri asked.

'Mmm,' she mumbled as if it was all she could muster as she laid on his chest, her eyes closed and a look of pure contentment on her face.

'Now you are mine forever, Lady Cinderella of house Tremaine,' Henri said formally, causing her to look over at him in shock.

Did she really think he wouldn't find out? He was too happy to be mad at her for keeping it from him. The trouble she would have saved them if she'd only been honest with him. The trouble he would have saved them if he'd only been honest with her.

'Tomorrow night at the ball, I'll introduce you to the world as my future wife.'

Tears sprung from her eyes and she smiled so brightly he couldn't help smiling back at her.

'Is this the part where I wake up?' she asked.

'My sweet Cinderella, I will spend the entire night proving to you that this is not a dream,' he said, a wicked smile touched his lips as he pinned her arms to the bed. He pressed his lips hungrily to hers.

He would spend his whole life proving it to her if he had to.

CHAPTER 16

Cinderella

The dress that Prince Henri gave Cinderella was a beautiful ball gown. The light blue seemed to make her eyes standout so stunningly that Cinderella had a hard time believing it was her own reflection staring back from the glass. It had been a long time since she had been allowed to be anything other than a servant, even in her own home.

The maid had left the room a short while ago but a nervous fluttering in her stomach had kept Cinderella glued to that spot in front of the mirror longer than expected. She looked down at the sparkling diamond on her finger and pictured Henri's smiling face. It was still hard to believe that this perfectly wicked prince had chosen her above all others. She took a deep breath to calm her nerves. Finally, she forced one foot in front of the other and headed for the ballroom.

The ball was already underway when she arrived, ladies swirled around the dancefloor in glittering gowns, their steps perfectly in sync to the tune of the orchestra. Prince Henri stood at the front of the room, his features showing his boredom quite clearly to all who cared to look upon him. Cinderella couldn't resist the smile tugging at her lips as she watched him greeting each eligible lady as she was presented to him, the king watching each interaction for even the smallest sign that the prince might take interest in one of them. A little satisfied warmth burrowed into her heart as he dismissed each of them with the same bored expression as the last.

Henri looked up from his bow and caught her eye, his eyebrow quirking up as he realised that she was watching him suffer through the process his father had insisted on. Henri stood, his spine straight, and he beckoned her to come with one elegant finger, his eyes never breaking away from hers. Part of her wondered if she should disobey him, no doubt he would have some delicious punishment for her if she did. But others were already looking at her and she wasn't sure Henri wouldn't mete out her punishment it in the middle of the ballroom, so she did as she was told.

All around her, whispers began to stir as the crowd of people wondered who she was to be receiving the special attentions of the prince. She could feel them creeping into her skin, bringing with them the viscous sting of self-doubt with each step she took until she was before Henri. She dipped into a low curtsey. 'Good evening, your highness,' she said graciously, not wanting to give the eligible ladies and their wagging tongues more fodder for their cannons.

'Will you greet me so coldly when we are wed?' Prince Henri asked, his voice a low growl. As she looked up at him, he took her hand and pulled her to him, causing a blush to rise to her cheeks as gasps echoed around the room. 'Dance with me. Save me from the endless torment of these desperate ladies,' he said, his lips so close to her ear that she felt a warmth stirring in her core.

Henri led her to the dancefloor and though the orchestra continued playing as though they hadn't noticed anything, the other couples had long since vacated the space to watch the show. Amongst the crowd, Cinderella noticed her stepmother staring at her, her gaze as critical and scrutinising as always. Realisation crossed her features and Cinderella knew she had been recognised. Panic made her heart race wildly in her chest.

'Everyone is staring at us,' she said self-consciously. Would her stepmother cause a scene? Would she call her out in front of all these people?

'Don't look at them, look at me,' Henri said, as though he couldn't believe she dared to look anywhere else.

Cinderella did as she was told, getting lost in his

intense gaze as her mind wandered to the way his lips felt on her skin, the way his hands explored her body, the way his skin felt against hers.

'What are you thinking about?' Henri asked, pulling her from her thoughts.

'Nothing,' she lied.

'Really? Because if you keep looking at me like that, I might just have to take you away from here.'

'Do you promise?' Cinderella asked, deciding to call him on his bluff. Well in part. She was also keen to get away from the glaring eyes of her stepmother and the jealous women who had hoped to trap the prince for themselves.

A look of surprise crossed Henri's face before desire darkened his eyes. 'You should know better than to challenge me, Princess,' he said. His husky voice rumbled through her, stoking her need.

Princess? Cinderella had hardly thought about the new title she would possess. It sounded strange to her ears. And soon other titles would come her way: wife, queen, mother. She wondered if the name her mother had given her would soon drift away from all memory entirely.

Henri suddenly signalled for the music to stop, and Cinderella was so caught up in her own thoughts that she nearly stepped on his foot. A hush fell over the entire room and the king leaned forward eagerly, his eyes lighting up at the sight of the ring on Cinderella's finger.

'I have an announcement to make,' Henri said, his voice echoing through the silent room. 'I have asked Lady Cinderella Tremaine for her hand and she has accepted.'

The men in the room quickly applauded, led by the enthusiastic clapping of the king himself, who thankfully didn't seem to recognise Cinderella from the day she'd attended the dining hall. But the ladies had a more half-hearted reaction, not that the king seemed to notice that, either. The king was positively beaming and Cinderella looked up at Henri with questioning eyes.

'Please don't ask,' he begged, and she thought she saw the tips of his ears turn pink for just a moment.

It was then that she caught her stepmother's eye, her expression dark and seething. Cinderella gripped Henri's hand a little tighter, even as she tried to convince herself that the woman couldn't do anything to her now.

'What is it?' Henri asked, turning to her with concern in his eyes.

'My stepmother is here,' she said hesitantly.

Henri's face hardened. 'We should have her removed, I hear the dungeons are lovely this time of year,' he said.

'No,' Cinderella said quickly, her eyes pleading. She didn't want to cause a scene. She didn't want to draw attention to her situation. She was sure that her stepmother wouldn't do anything. If she announced that Cinderella was a servant, she would have to explain why a lady had been degraded in such a way and be forever shamed. For the first time in her life, Cinderella had won. She wondered if her stepmother regretted the way she had treated her now. If she had been a proper mother, she would be about to move into the palace, but now she would stay exactly as she was while Cinderella got everything she ever wanted. But Cinderella couldn't help feeling sad at the thought. She'd never wanted revenge, she'd only ever wanted her stepmother to love her as her own.

'Fine,' Henri reluctantly agreed and it warmed Cinderella's heart that he was so ready to come to her rescue. She had finally found the love she had always dreamed of, a love like her mother and father had. 'But you, my dear wife, have taken your eyes off me again. I think you need to learn who you belong to,' Henri said, squeezing her hand.

'What?' Cinderella asked, panic seeping into her voice. That wicked smile had stretched lazily across his lips and that was usually followed by something devious.

The music struck up again and the dancefloor filled with couples once more. Henri danced Cinderella through them all until they were at the entrance. He took her hand in his and darted through the doors before anyone could notice them leave, or perhaps he simply didn't care if they were seen. Cinderella's heart raced as she was dragged through the palace to a familiar room. A room she had once been forced to spend a great deal of time in as a servant. Henri shut the door firmly behind them.

'Is it really alright for us to leave the ball so soon?' Cinderella asked.

'You expect me to worry about that when you look so beautiful?' Henri asked. He pressed his lips to her neck, sending a shiver of pleasure through her. 'I told you I would show you who you belong to.'

A blush rose to Cinderella's cheeks. How could he say such things with a straight face? For once she wished that she could make him blush. She knew that was an impossible feat, though. She didn't have the confidence to pull off something so bold that would cause the prince to blush.

'But –' she began to protest but the pleasure from his lips on her neck, his hands on her body made her voice breathy and she stopped herself. She could feel him growing hard against her and she couldn't remember why she wanted him to stop. She never wanted him to stop.

'You should just give in,' Henri said, closing the distance between them and pressing her back against the wall. 'You've lost this round,' he said before bringing his lips to her neck, each delectable kiss sending a burst of warmth into her skin.

'Have I?' she asked, her voice filled with desire. 'Or am I getting exactly what I want?'

'Are you now?' Henri asked as he pushed her dress

over her hips, letting it drop to the floor. His lips captured hers hungrily and she wrapped her arms around his neck, pushing her fingers through his hair as she surrendered to the need that was growing inside her.

Henri guided her arms down, his hands sliding along her skin as he pushed her slip from her shoulders, letting it fall to the ground with her dress. His hands continued to glide over her skin, massaging her breasts, sliding over her hips, cupping her arse. His mouth descended on her breast, he took one taut nipple between his teeth, flicking his tongue over the hardened nub, causing her back to arch in pleasure.

'Henri!' she moaned, her muscles clenching in anticipation. She slid her hand slowly down his torso until she reached the bulge in his pants. He hissed out a breath as she stroked him.

Henri released her and pulled out of her reach. 'Get on the bed,' he ordered, his voice rough with desire. Cinderella did as she was told with the sound of clothes hitting the floor behind her. She laid on the bed as instructed and Henri pulled two silk ties out of a drawer next to the bed. 'What –?' she began but her lips were quickly sealed with his to prevent her from asking questions. When he was sure she wouldn't ask questions, he pulled away from her again and tied each of her wrists to the bedhead with the strips of silk.

'Do you trust me?' he asked before dropping a kiss to her neck.

'Mm,' she moaned as his lips trailed down her skin, his tongue flicking over her nipple, his hands sliding along her curves. She was wet and wanting and he knew it. His lips trailed lower, lower, until he came to the apex of her thighs. She reflexively drew her knees together but he forced her legs apart with his hands as his lips sucked at her clitoris.

'Ah, Henri!' she cried out. A tingling sensation shot through her as his tongue expertly licked at her, her toes curling in pleasure as his tongue dipped inside her, her body squirming against him. The pressure was building inside her and he continued to lick at her, suck at her, dip his tongue inside of her until she cried out, her body writhing with the force of the orgasm that he greedily lapped at until she fell still.

'Who do you belong to?' he asked, positioning himself on top of her, the slick head of his erection teasing her entrance.

'You,' she breathed.

He pushed into her, thrusting deep until her back arched and she called out his name in a wanton voice. 'Fuck,' he grunted as he picked up speed. He hooked an arm behind her knee, opening her up to him. Her cries echoed through the room as she came on his cock, her muscles clenching around him, milking him until he came inside her.

He kissed her neck, her lips, her jaw, as he untied her wrists. Finally free, Cinderella snuggled into him, resting her head on his chest as she listened to the racing of his heart with a contented smile.

'I love you,' he said as his thumb drew small circles on her arm.

Cinderella's heart soared at the words. She couldn't wait to marry this man, to be bound to him for eternity. There was nowhere else she would rather be.

'I love you, too.'

EPILOGUE

Cinderella stood outside her old house. It had only been six months since she'd left it but it felt like a lifetime had passed. She rang the bell with a gloved hand and waited for it to be answered. She had no doubt that the occupants of the house were already well aware that she was standing there.

The person who answered the door was a meek little thing, no doubt treated poorly by Lucinda and her daughters. Cinderella felt pity for her but forced herself to keep her head high and not think of such things.

The girl's eyes grew wide and she curtsied low. 'Your 'ighnesses,' she said and ushered them inside. Cinderella offered her a kind smile before she led them down the hallway to the parlour.

She wondered how long her stepmother would

make her wait. She surely still hated her, even more so now that she was a princess. But there was a certain amount of respect she was now forced to afford Cinderella.

Even so, Cinderella's stomach flipped nervously.

Lucinda appeared only moments later, with Prudence and Gertrude in tow, both of them looking like they'd sucked on sour grapes.

'Cinderella, what an unexpected surprise,' Lucinda said.

'I believe you are forgetting decorum, Lady Tremaine,' Henri said, his voice almost a growl. That protective side of him was showing itself again, and Cinderella was glad to have that on her side.

'It doesn't matter,' Cinderella said, placing a hand gently on his arm. Henri looked as if he disagreed but he kept his thoughts to himself. 'I'm here to collect my things, stepmother,' she continued.

'Well, there isn't much in this house that belongs to you, so that shouldn't take much time at all,' Lucinda said, her smile sickeningly sweet.

'Actually, we have a copy of your late husband's will, Madam,' Henri said, holding up an envelope containing the document.

Lucinda's face paled.

'Yes. My dear Henri told me that I should kick you out of the house,' Cinderella said, playing up the fact that she was now married to the prince her stepsisters had so coveted. She was a nice person but she wasn't a saint. 'But as I know you don't have anywhere else to go, and, well, I won't be living in this house, so I've decided to let you stay. You may rent it from me.'

'What?' Lucinda demanded, rage causing her body to shake.

Cinderella couldn't quite supress her satisfied smile. 'It's a perfectly reasonable proposal. I will give you until the end of the week to decide. For now, the movers are here to collect my things. There's so much to go through,' she said, flashing her stepmother a happy smile before flouncing out of the room to begin her work.

Henri followed her out and wrapped his arms around her. 'I think you enjoyed that a little more than someone with your goodness should,' he whispered in her ear, his breath tickling her neck.

'What can I say? I think you're rubbing off on me.'

'Are you sure you won't miss it? It is your home, after all.'

Cinderella shook her head. 'No, it hasn't been my home for a long time now. My home is wherever you are.'

'You're going to give me a cavity, if you keep that up,' he said, but she caught the slightly pink tinge to his cheeks and couldn't resist laughing. Each day she seemed to see new parts of him, and each day she was thankful that fate had led her to him.

ABOUT THE AUTHOR

Lorelei Johnson is an Australian author who writes tantalising romances that will leave you wanting more.

While Lorelei typically writes paranormal romance, she will sometimes stray from that path to venture into the unexpected.

In her collection you'll find a variety of seductive romances featuring swoon-worthy men and feisty women. You're bound to find the HEA you're looking for.

BOOKS BY LORELEI JOHNSON

Tantalising Tales Collection

My Sweet Cinderella

Scarlett and the Wolf

Beauty and the Beast

The Touch of Snow

The Little Mermaid

Summoned by the Piper

Rumpelstiltskin

Loved by the Zodiac

Loved by Aries

Embraced by Scorpio

Printed in Great Britain
by Amazon